Daddy's Naughty Gangster

An ABDL age play romantic story about a college student who finds love with her Daddy Dom and herself as the game changer in his organized crime family

By Tina Moore

Table of Contents

Chapter 1

Lucy had graduated top of her class. Her first preference of College had accepted her, and she worked at one of the campus canteens. But like most students, Lucy was broke. After paying for her lodgings, groceries, and phone bill, there wasn't a penny left. She had tried tutoring other students, working extra shifts at work and had even reduced her grocery shopping to a mere $45 a week and yet, at the end of every month, she still came up skint. With the burden of her four-year course still ahead of her, Lucy decided it was time she branched out and got creative.

The following day, she spent the afternoon in her dorm room, searching the internet for different ways she could earn some easy cash. The things she saw made her wonder just how sheltered a life she had really experienced. From finding a website where she could sell her used panties for $50 a pop, to being an adult text chat operator, Lucy had wondered why she had never thought of looking online for jobs before. *Maybe I can get a sugar Daddy or something*; Lucy thought as she created a profile on an interest dating site. She filled in the required sections, uploaded a photo, and waited. Sitting on her bed, she brought her knees to her chest and placed her head on top of her knees. Hearing her phone buzz almost instantly, Lucy frowned in confusion as she saw she had received a message from *DADDY486*.

Hi, I'm Mason, you look cute, little one. I want to see more of you. The message read. Lucy looked at her phone and wondered how she should reply. *It's not like I have to hide the fact I'm looking for his money, the site is called SugarDaddies.com*, Lucy thought as she began to reply.

Thanks, Lucy typed, entirely at a loss for what to write next.

I can see that you are shy, why don't you tell me a little bit about yourself. I'll go first. I'm 36 and from out of town but have recently moved here for work. I like to keep fit; I'm in the local football team. We aren't very good, just a bunch of guys kicking the ball around really but it's still fun. Maybe you can come and watch sometime. I've got a dog called Huxley, he is a boxer cross mastiff but is a big sook even though he looks scary, Mason replied. Lucy read the message and couldn't believe that she was messaging with this stranger, but smiled as she typed back.

Hey Mason, I'm Lucy. Huxley sounds really sweet. I'm actually studying really close to where you are; I hadn't realized we were so close in location. Have you done this before? Like had a sugar baby? Lucy messaged. She waited for a reply, but when didn't come she messaged the three other men who had contacted her in the time she had been messaging with Mason.

After two hours of constant messaging, she put her phone down. Her head was a frenzy of photos, allowance offers, and sexy messages that had made her wet with desire. Looking up reasons for being ghosted by people online, Lucy took out a box of crackers and read about the troubles sugar babies had experienced and tried to learn as much as she could, just as Mason messaged her back.

Hey, sorry Lucy, I had to quickly get some papers graded that were due back last week. I haven't had to manage my time for a while so I might be a bit rusty at the start as I get back into the swing of making sure you've got everything you need, Mason replied, making Lucy's pussy instantly tingle.

That's ok; I had thought you didn't want to talk anymore, so thanks for the heads up. Do you have time to talk now? Lucy asked back, holding her breath and smiling when Mason answered.

Yeah, little one, how about you tell me the kind of thing you are looking for and I'll answer those questions you asked earlier, Mason replied as Lucy lay back on her bed and began texting him.

Lucy stayed up all night, learning how Mason had recently got his new job but that he would be transferring departments in the fall. He told her about his past relationships, explaining how some sugar babies and daddies are just scammers, and that he was willing to pay $2000 a week in allowance. Lucy couldn't believe that someone would want to give their hard-earned money away, but she was grateful that Mason seemed to get off on the idea of paying for someone else.

So, like, what do you want from this then? Lucy asked, her eyes growing weary as the time neared midnight.

Well, that's a bit of a loaded question. Now, I just want to let you know right now that if you aren't completely happy to do these things, this won't work out between us ok? Mason wrote making Lucy bite her lip. She nodded her head even though Mason couldn't see her as she saw that he was writing and waited for his response.

I want you to be my submissive. I want a girl who enjoys being teased and tormented before she gets fucked until I am satisfied. And when you aren't my little slut, I want you in diapers. I want to dress you up as a baby and make you drink from a bottle. I want to spank you when you are bad and tie you up so you can't escape from me. I want you to call me, Daddy, and I want you to be my little girl, I want to control the things you wear, the time you go to bed. I want to know the places you go when you aren't in your dorm room, and I want to be able to take you on lavish holidays, Mason explained, making Lucy's eyes grew wide.

You'll send me photos of you wearing the clothes I buy for you and send to you; you'll wear a diaper to bed and send me photo's of that too. We will skype, and you'll show me your pussy before I make you wear a chastity belt under the diaper you'll wear during the day. And if you are a good girl for Daddy, I'll let you cum over webcam, Mason continued, making Lucy freeze. She had never been spoken to like this before; she didn't know how to reply. So she just stared at her phone as the messages came pouring in.

When you aren't my little princess, you'll still call me Daddy. You'll take my cock whenever I stick it in you without resisting. I can't wait to be sitting on the couch with you, the tip of my cock in your mouth as we watch a movie, your tongue licking it lazily while I play with your tits, was the next message Lucy read, her mouth opening in surprise.

You're going to love my big sack too, my balls are always full, and I can just imagine how you'll feel sitting on my lap with my cock up you and your ass squishing on my big sack, it's like a pillow. But you'll feel that when I make you take one ball in your mouth at a time, Mason messaged. Lucy just read the messages over and over, surprised at how horny she was becoming reading the things Mason wanted to do with her.

Of course, having you fight me a little bit is always hot. But you shouldn't make too much of a fuss, especially when we are in public and I unzip my pants and lock you in place with my hard rod spreading your puffy pussy open. People might see, and Daddy doesn't want to share his little girl. Something else I like to do is tie you to a suspended X above my bed and spear your cunt with my cock, forcing you to take it as I buck up into you. That's so hot, your pussy will drip onto my cock, and you won't be able to stop me as I plow you. I'll probably have suction cups on your titties too making them sensitive and a gag in your mouth. Yeah, I can just see that now, all bound and open, having to accept where I want to stuff you. Maybe it'll be your ass; perhaps it'll be your pussy, you won't know until I am rubbing your clit and shooting my cum up you, Mason continued, making Lucy wriggle in bed as she read the filth he was sending her.

You like it when Daddy sends you dirty messages, don't you, sweetheart. I bet your pussy is dripping wet; I bet you are trying to stop your juices from wetting your panties. I want you to show Daddy, show me the moist patch on your panties, Mason instructed. Lucy was surprised how her thighs parted at his request as she lowered her phone and lifted up her skirt to take a photo of her light blue panties with the damp patch beginning to show through. Sending it to Mason, Lucy held her breath, hoping that he liked it as she felt her phone vibrate almost instantly.

Oh, Daddy likes, came the message that made Lucy press her panties into her cunt, making them even wetter and sending him a new photo.

You are a dirty girl, aren't you, baby? Mason asked in a new message.

Yes, Daddy, replied Lucy, smoothing her skirt back down over her cum soaked panties.

I don't want this to end, but I guess it needs to so that you can get to sleep, little girl. Tomorrow you'll receive a little reward over that secure money exchange site you mentioned; I'll set up an account on there while you are sleeping tonight. I'm assuming it'll be there by morning. Sweet dreams, little one, Mason said, making Lucy feel a yearning in her heart as his status changed to offline. Looking at the time on her phone, she rolled her eyes. The communal showers would be closed by now; she would have to sleep in her wet panties all night. She thought about changing them but liked that they were dirty because of what Mason had said to her and decided to keep them on. Changing into her short pajama shorts and racerback pink singlet, she traced her nipples under her blankets thinking about what Mason had said, how it would feel to have him suction her titties while he fucked her exposed cunt.

Falling asleep with her phone between her thighs pressing against her cunt, and not feeling the vibrations of her phone making her clit hard through the night, Lucy dreamt of sucking Mason's cock and feeling his generous sack soft against her lips. Waking to her phone vibrating on her clit, Lucy found that she was sucking her thumb as she looked around nervously, hoping that her dorm mate hadn't seen her. Surprised when she looked over to see that she had never come home, Lucy reached between her thighs and rubbed herself before realizing that her phone was still vibrating.

Good morning little baby, Daddy had fun last night, look at the wood you gave me thinking of you this morning, Mason had messaged. Lucy looked at his cock and blushed.   *I just want you inside of me now,* Lucy involuntarily replied, her fingers messaging him back before she had realized she had. She looked at his cock and didn't know dicks could look so good. He had pulled back his foreskin, exposing his wet mushroom head that looked like it would need to slither slowly up and down her full pussy lips to spread her open. His thick girth making her suck her bottom lip. He had been right about his sack. Lucy had never seen balls like this before. As his cock lifted up, Lucy saw how his sack was full like he had said, with two clearly defined balls exposed.

Yeah, I'd love to see you choking on this fat knob, running your tongue up and down Daddy's long schlong. You're going to spread those ass cheeks for Daddy's big thumper and take it like the cum dumpster you are, aren't you Lucy? Mason text.

I'm going to bone you till you need Daddy to carry you around campus, so everyone sees that you are my little cock taking princess, he added before Lucy's roommate walked into the room and startled her. Lucy was happy that her roommate was too busy collapsing on her bed after another wild night partying to notice that Lucy's hand had been down her panties, the same dirty pair she had worn all night. Leaving her phone buried in her blankets, Lucy grabbed her toiletry bag and quickly walked to the cupboard, grabbed her clothes, and walked to the bathroom.

Chapter 2

Lucy tried to concentrate on the lecture she had somehow managed to make on-time. The professor was talking about something she had never heard of before, and she knew she needed to pass this class. It was her weakest subject, and although her grades from the other subjects had carried her through the semester, this was the one that would have her passing the semester or not. She had turned her phone off, but as the professor rambled on, all she could think about was Mason and the dirty messages she knew he would be sending her. She had told him she needed to study, and he had told her that it was her problem and not his, that he was going to message her continually all day until she was so desperate to be fucked that she showed him her pussy online that very night.

Don't you dare touch your sluty little cunt

baby girl, that's Daddy's now, and I'll tell you when you can touch it. Tonight, pretty baby, tonight you'll show Daddy your pussy. Your Daddy demands it; Mason wrote before she had turned her phone off and hurried into the amphitheater. Lucy wrote down some notes as she thought back to how Mason had said he would deposit her some money on her account as a way of starting their dynamic, and turning her phone back on, Lucy was excited to see if he had done so or not. Trying not to moan at the latest of Mason's messages, Lucy flicked through her phone to see that he had, in fact, sent her $500 with a note attached to the payment.

I hope this finds you well, my darling. It was a far cry from the vulgar messages he had assaulted her phone with, the types that had kept her desperate and horny all day. Looking down to see he had messaged again, Lucy read it before clenching her cunt shut, trying to stop the dripping of cum she could feel escaping her.

I'm going to keep my fat snake filling you as you bend over in front of me and wiggle your ass for

Daddy, once you've been a good girl and done that for me, maybe I'll let you get off your tippy toes, but unlikely. What is more likely is that I turn you around, push you onto your knees and not let you go until you've drunk all Daddy's milk up. Lucy squeezed her knees shut and practically jumped up when the lecture ended racing back to her room and diving under her bed covers as she sighed and rubbed her pussy feverously. *Oh my god, I need to cum, he won't know if I do or not, oh my god, I want him inside of me,* she thought as she began rubbing her clit harder, moaning as she got herself off, happy to finally be alone with her cunt.

"Hi Lucy, nice to finally be able to hear your voice," Mason said three hours later. Lucy had been nervous to see him, worried that she wouldn't find him attractive but as he sat talking to her through her laptop screen, she knew that she had nothing to worry about. In truth, it was her that had started to feel nervous that Mason wouldn't like her. She had dark brown hair that was cut in a trendy style, blue eyes, and an angelic-looking face. Her breasts were one size too big for her body, making her look bustier than she was. Her 5'6 height was fairly average, but her ass had always made her feel self-conscious. The boys at her high school used to call her bootylicious because when she wore sports leggings, her ass would jiggle like a stripper's. She looked at Mason's handsome face, the way he rolled the sleeves up of his button-down business shirt and the gold chain around his neck, growing wet all over again.

"Hey, yeah, it is nice," Lucy replied nervously. Mason liked how she blushed; it turned him on to see her so willing but so timid.

"Did you like the messages I sent you today?" He asked cheekily, a grin forming on the right side of his mouth. Lucy watched as Mason stood up, flexing his hips forward in front of the camera showing off his monster bulge against his handsome business trousers.

"Because I sure enjoyed thinking about you

in all those positions and situations," he said. Lucy couldn't see his face; all she could see was his throbbing cock moving under his pants.

"Do you want to say hello to Daddy's big boy, it's important to me that you two are friends," Mason said, pulling on the buckle of his belt with both his hands, pushing his bulge closer to the camera as jiggling it.

"Yes please, Daddy," Lucy found herself saying, the words escaping her lips before she could stop them. Mason chuckled as he pulled open his belt, unbuttoned the top of his trousers and slowly unzipped his pants. Lucy could see the well-fitting grey briefs that housed his thick snake as he pushed through the opening that he had just made and began stroking himself.

"Open your mouth for me, stick your tongue out," Mason instructed, he could still see Lucy although her only vision was of the fat rod he began to pull on. He took his time, shaking his cock in front of the camera before pulling it up as his balls fell out of his briefs.

"This is going to be your new best friend," Mason said, watching as Lucy kept her mouth open and her tongue out, saliva beginning to drip onto her t-shirt.

"I didn't say you could swallow," Mason said as Lucy tried to close her mouth, not used to the feeling of fighting her natural instincts. Mason didn't have to jerk himself for long until he was stiff with the head of his cock, pointing angrily towards the camera.

"He likes you, shake your titties for me," Mason instructed, watching as Lucy obediently shook her huge rack for him.

"Play with them over your shirt," Mason said, smiling as Lucy lifted her hands to her breasts and began groping them. Squeezing them together and following Mason's orders, Lucy leaned back in her chair and put her feet up on her desk, exposing her pussy for him.

"That's a girl. Stroke that pussy for Daddy. I want to fill your dirty little cunt with a nice big load of Daddy cream. You're lucky you're on that side of the computer, or you'd be forced to let me face fuck you hard, like a good girl," Mason said as Lucy stroked her moistening slit.

"Pull your panties off and then get back into that position," Mason said, seeing Lucy disappear only to re-emerge again, this time pushing her skirt between her thighs to hide her pussy from Mason.

"Show Daddy," Mason instructed, his balls filling the palm of his large hand as he jerked his cock with the other.

"Like this, Daddy?" Lucy said, spreading her legs open further and slowly pulling up her skirt. Mason exploded onto the camera the instant he saw Lucy's pussy. Her puffy pink lips looked like velvet, and her glistening hole made him grunt with delight as he gripped his cock hard, wanting to be inside of her. He wiped the camera clean. He sat back down in his chair and shook his head in disbelief.

"And you don't have a boyfriend or anyone fucking you right now?" he asked, feeling his cock throb.

"No," Lucy said, shaking her head, her titties jiggling as she did so.

"Hey, Daddy," Lucy said confidently, leaning forward and taking her top off. Mason watched as two huge globes popped out from the bottom of Lucy's tight band t-shirt, cupped in a black lace bra.

"Oh, the things I'm going to do to you," Mason said, laughing at how turned on he was.

"Play with your titties. Show me your nipples," Mason instructed, watching as Lucy's pink rosebud nipples emerged from her bra. Lucy licked her fingers and rubbed them over her nipples, making then hard as Mason smiled, thinking of how he would tease them until she was begging him to stop.

"You'll need to wear a bra under your onesie, little girl, I don't want those huge titties to hurt your back," Mason said.

"What's your size?" He added, opening an internet search, excited to buy her lingerie.

"Um, I actually don't really know, I've never been measured, I kind of just go with what fits," Lucy replied, blushing and looking down, so her hair fell from behind her ear.

"Well. When you feel comfortable meeting up, we can go lingerie shopping and get you fitted properly. I have to look after my little one," Mason said.

"Thank you, Daddy," Lucy replied, lifting her head and tucking her hair behind her ear again.

"Daddy, I think I need to go, my dormmate is meant to be finishing her lecture right now, she'll be home any minute," Lucy said, wanting to dress herself again, worried that she would be found out with her pussy exposed to the computer.

"That's alright, sweetie. Thank you so much for chatting with me this afternoon. You are so beautiful, Lucy. I think we can make each other very happy," Mason said, laughing as Lucy quickly turned the camera off just as she saw the door to her room open. Running toward her bed, Lucy pulled the covers back and jumped into the bed, breathing deeply under the covers.

Chapter 3

Lucy had narrowly escaped getting caught out by diving into her bed and pretending to be reading a book by the time her dormmate walked into their room.

"Hey," she casually said, as she fell on her own bed and began to flip through a magazine.

"Hi, how was your day?" Lucy said, trying to act normal as her sheets were made wet with the cum that leaked from her cunt onto her soft flannel bed sheets.

"Yeah, it was like whatever. Want to go out tonight?" Ella asked. Lucy had never been invited to a party before, and she blushed not knowing how to act at one.

"Um, I think I'll just stay in, I've got a paper I need to finish," Lucy replied, trying to sound cool.

"Suit yourself," Ella said, flicking her perfect red hair from one side to the next before standing up and walking back out of the room. Signing in relief for not getting caught out, Lucy quickly got up and locked the door.

"Daddy, I can't wait to meet you in person," Lucy said down the phone the following evening. She had spoken with Mason for the last hour as she sat an off-campus internet lounge and watched as the hipsters typed furiously on their laptops. *I wonder if any of them are actually doing anything important,* Lucy thought.

"It'll be really lovely. We can go for ice cream and walk by the river. We'll go off-campus, so no one gives you questioning looks," Mason replied. With the allowance, Mason had already given Lucy she had a bought new laptop and was looking through his social media accounts as they spoke.

"Did you really win a beer-chugging comp?" Lucy laughed.

"Yes, I have many talents, that is one of them," Mason said, amused that Lucy was such a curious person.

"Look, baby girl, Daddy, has to go unfortunately but I'll see you tomorrow, alright?" Mason said, causing Lucy to have a knot in her tummy. She didn't want him to go; she wanted to stay with him forever.

"Ok, see you tomorrow, Daddy," Lucy said, smiling as she ended the conversation.

Lucy stayed sitting in the café, watching the people who came in and out. She looked at the way the people interacted and wondered why she never felt like she fit in. *At least with Mason, I feel normal,* she thought deciding to buy a takeaway latte before leaving.

Walking out onto the street, Lucy walked passed the tall buildings with people in fancy suits and the usual mundane city scene. Trains screeching, pigeons searching for crumbs, a deafening noise that reduced everything to silence. *If I lay down here and never moved, no one would even notice,* Lucy thought. She reached into her backpack and took out her earphones, connecting them to her phone and playing a song that seemed to be screaming from her heart. *I wonder what Mason would think if he knew I felt like this. I wonder if he is trying to numb something with this whole sugar Daddy thing as well*, Lucy said to herself sitting on the river bank. She watched the ferries drive past, making ripples in the water, wondering when she would feel something, anything. That was what Mason was for her and she knew it. He was something to explore, a break in the pattern, the pattern that forced itself to play on a loop in her head. The backlash of a hand, the surprise she felt when she learned the world wasn't as she thought it would be. Pulling out a blade of grass, Lucy saw the mountain she needed to climb and wished like hell someone could make the trip for her. *What's the point? When everyone just leaves, will the dream be worth the nightmare? Will it hurt more than the other times, or will somehow this miracle of a man be who I've been searching for*, Lucy asked herself, wanting answers to questions she didn't know how to word.

"Hey baby," Mason said the next day at the spot they had decided to meet. Lucy smiled as he took her hand in his and kissed it before pulling her into his arms.

"You smell yummy," he added, smelling her scent of sweet candy and berries.

"Thanks," Lucy said, nervous and not knowing what to say next.

"Come on, let's go," Mason said kindly. He could see she was nervous and wanted to get her somewhere familiar so she might relax.

"Do you want to hold Daddy's hand?" Mason asked, smiling warmly at Lucy, who just nodded her head.

"Yes, Daddy," Lucy almost whispered. Mason opened his hand to her, and she watched as she placed her hand in his, hoping that she wasn't being a fool and falling for someone who was just going to leave her.

"What is your favorite flavor, baby girl?' Mason asked as they approached the ice cream store.

"I love choc mint. Which one do you like the best?" Lucy said while Mason held the door open for her.

"Choc fudge twist," he replied, leading her to the chairs at the side of the store. A waitress came over to their table, a waitress Lucy blushed at when she saw her.

"Hey Lucy, cute outfit," Ella said as she eyed Mason. Mason looked at a startled Lucy and rubbed her foot under the table, taking her by surprise.

"Thanks, Ella," Lucy half mumbled as Mason looked at her apologetically. This was the last thing he wanted, to have Lucy closed off and nervous around him.

"We will take two sundaes, one with choc mint and the other choc fudge twist thanks," Mason said, turning back to Lucy, signaling that he was finished with Ella.

"Coming right up," Ella said as she turned on her heel and happily walked back to the counter to make their order.

"Lucy, are you alright, sweetie?" Mason asked Lucy, who was clearly not alright. Lucy just shook her head and bit her bottom lip.

"That's my roommate," she whispered, looking down and trying to hide her embarrassment.

"Are you embarrassed to be here with me?" Mason asked. Although he was over a decade older than Lucy was, he looked good for his age. With dark brown hair and a handsome face with eyes that could make the naughtiest of girls submit. He had worn tan boots, denim jeans and a white t-shirt, a tan jacket with the sleeves rolled up. He was the type of man who made woman double-take, and who made husbands jealous that his dominance outdid theirs. He had hoped that Lucy wouldn't feel embarrassed about being with him, and he felt intrigued as to why he worried about his appearance with her when he rarely felt self-conscious.

"No, it's not that at all. It's that, what if she

finds out that you and I are," Lucy said, trailing off and looking at her sundae Ella put in front of her.

"Thanks," Mason said, smiling politely at Ella.

"I put an extra cherry on yours," Ella whispered in Mason's ear, pretending she was wiping the table down.

"Oh, I don't like cherries," Mason said, annoyed that she was such a flirt. Mason looked at Ella in the eye before raising an eyebrow, dismissing her with a flick of his head

"I thought you told me you liked them?" Lucy questioned, referring to one of their previous conversations.

"I do, but not from her," Mason said, making Lucy laugh and reach out for his hand to hold.
They finished their sundaes as the afternoon sun began to go down, creating a sky of pink and purple.

"Are you ready to go, baby?" Mason asked as he took out his wallet.

"It's ok, Daddy, I can pay," Lucy said which

only made Mason laugh.

"Baby girl," Mason said, coming over to sit next to Lucy. He wrapped his arm around her, feeling how she fitted perfectly into his embrace, her breasts pushing into his torso as he held her.

"Daddy also pays," Mason said, kissing Lucy on her forehead. As Mason got up to leave, Ella came over with a milkshake on her tray, picked up their glasses before pretending to slip and pouring the milkshake all over Lucy. Lucy froze, her eyes being to tear up as Mason turned around to see what had happened. Shocked, he walked back, being at Lucy's side in seconds.

"You stupid bitch, look what you have done," Mason growled. He pushed Ella out of the way and went to get napkins, cleaning Lucy and kissing her on her cheek.

"It's ok little one, Daddy will get you some new clothes," Mason whispered into Lucy's ear. Standing up and walking over to Ella, he reached out and ripped the magnetic badge from her outfit.

"You're fired," Mason said, making the girl

roll her eyes.

"You're not the manager, you can't fire me," Ella said in a bratty voice.

"No, I'm not the manager, I am the owner, and I don't want sluts like you in my shop," Mason said, before walking out of the store with Lucy following behind him.

"Daddy, do you really own the store?" Lucy asked, excepting the jacket, Mason draped over her shoulders.

"Yes, baby girl. Daddy owns a lot of real estate," Mason said, walking her quickly to a luxury clothing store Lucy would have never even dreamed of going into by herself.

"Daddy, I'm all dirty, I can't go in there," Lucy said, self-conscious and blushing.

"Baby girl, you see this card?" Mason said, opening up his wallet and showing Lucy a black Amex. Lucy raised her eyebrow; she didn't understand what it meant.

"When I leave this card on their counter, just watch how they spoil you," Mason said, enjoying Lucy's puzzled face. He smirked as he took her hand and led her into the store, ignoring the snobby retail assistants and going straight to the counter. He pulled out his card, put in on the counter like he had told Lucy he would do and eyed the woman with the tight bun, and pulled back smile that looked more like a snarl.

"We are going to need champagne, chocolates and something worth spending money on for this little one. Oh, and close the store, I don't want to be interrupted when I smash your sales goals for the month," Mason said, watching how the woman's eye lit up with the unlimited limit the card held, knowing that her commission would be considerable.

"Right away, Sir," she said, walking swiftly from behind the counter and taking Lucy by her hand. She clicked her fingers at the other woman who quickly locked the doors of the store. The woman led Lucy into a changing room, as Mason sat on one of the large chairs as he waited for his champagne. He looked around the store and sighed a contented sigh while he watched the women dress Lucy in couture. Looking around the store, he got up and went to the belts, wallets, and travel luggage. Seeing nothing that took his interest, he walked back over to where Lucy was changing.

"Maybe we should get you some new lingerie today as well, darling?" Mason suggested, watching as the women scurried off to find her sets of emerald green and deep red.

"Daddy, this is too much. I don't even know when I would wear something like this," Lucy whispered, looking down at the elegant shoes the assistants were buckling to her ankles.

"I guess it's not really college-friendly, is it? How about we get you a few nice outfits, then go somewhere else, somewhere they sell a little more, street style? That way you'll have something for every occasion?" Mason said, dismissing the new heels an assistant was showing Lucy.

"I'd love that, thank you, Daddy," Lucy said, once the assistants had gone to ring up their purchases. Amongst five pairs of heels, Mason had also bought Lucy three complete outfits, two scarves, four jackets, and two lingerie sets. That had been his favorite, watching as the women had measured Lucy, watching her little face burn red at the touch of another woman. He had also got her two travel bags, a laptop case, keyring, and a phone case. Ringing his assistant to come and collect the items for Lucy, with strict instruction to take them to Mason's house, they paid for the items and left the store. Lucy held Mason's hand as they walked down the street, feeling self-conscious that people were staring at her.

"It's because they want to be you, darling. They wish they could look as beautiful as you," Mason said, kissing the top of Lucy's head and holding her to his side. As they walked from store to store, purchasing boots, sneakers, a new phone for Lucy as well as some gadgets Mason insisted she needed like a camera drone and new wireless earphones, Lucy wondered just how much real estate Mason owned to be able to shop like this.

"Ok, little one, last stop. Makeup and jewelry," Mason said to a tired Lucy. She had never had a day like this in her life, and as the night sky began to fall, Lucy rested her head on Mason's shoulder as the car drove them to the next strip of stores.

"You're very quiet little girl, had Daddy worn you out?" Mason said, loving that Lucy was cuddling into him. She just nodded as she yawned and sleepily looked up at him.

"Yes, Daddy," she said before sucking her thumb. Mason placed his hand on her cheek and stroked her with his thumb affectionately.

"Maybe we should get you home then. Would you like to come to my house and let me get you ready for bed, little girl?" Mason replied, adjusting the headband Lucy now wore. She just nodded her head and closed her eyes again as Mason lifted her onto his lap and cradled her in his loving arms. He smiled down at her, happy that she didn't care about missing out on the final stage of their shopping spree and rocked her gently as their driver drove them home.

Chapter 4

When they arrived at Mason's house, Lucy was already fast asleep. It was near 7:30 pm and the overwhelming day had caught Lucy off guard. As Mason's door was opened for him, he exited the car, Lucy laying like a princess in his arms as his driver smiled at him.

"You have a beautiful girl there, Sir," the older man said. Having been Mason's driver for more than ten years, he had seen many a girl Mason had brought home. He had seen the girl's in the early days, the gold-digging ones who had been brats. He had seen the shy girls, who Mason had introduced to the DDlg lifestyle only to have them run off with another Daddy once they had learned what they liked about the kink. He had even seen the girl who had tried to blackmail Mason, which had almost cost him his fortune. But he had never seen Mason care for a girl the way he seemed to care for Lucy.

"She is something special, Alfred," Mason said, before motioning to the back seat where he had been previously sitting.

"There's something for you and Cherry in the back; I hope she will forgive me for ripping you out of the family BBQ today. I wasn't expecting to need you. Have the next two days off, I have a feeling I'm going to be staying at home this weekend," Mason said. He had bought Alfred a bottle of expensive Champagne and a new watch, the same type Mason himself owned. As for Alfred's wife Cherry, she was always harder to buy for as she thought Mason's luxurious lifestyle was wasteful and was not afraid to let Mason know her feelings. He had loved their jokes, Cherry always complaining Mason didn't do enough for charity and Mason continually reminding her that he gave away millions to charity every year. Today, as a thank you for understanding that Alfred's loyalty was to Mason first and foremost, Mason had bought her a new trench coat, scarf, and sunglasses, knowing that their joke of him one day being able to buy her love would cause her to smirk with satisfaction upon seeing her gifts.

"Oh, Sir. This is too much. Thank you. Cherry won't be able to stay mad at you for very long this time," Alfred laughed, beaming up at Mason. Mason smiled, a tear almost escaping his eye, and Alfred just shook his head.

"No need to say it, Sir," Alfred said, touching Mason's shoulder and nodding goodnight to him. Mason walked up to the front steps of his home, the door opening for him as his butler waited patiently by the door as Mason watched Alfred drive out of the lavish grounds.

"Good evening, Sir, your instructions have been followed accordingly," the butler said as Mason passed him.

"Thank you, have a bath run in the master will you," Mason said, carrying Lucy up the alabaster stairwell and along the hallway to his room. Placing Lucy down on his king-sized bed, he watched as she slowly opened her eyes. Startling slightly, Lucy looked around the room.

"Daddy?" She said in a worried tone, relieved when Mason jumped into bed beside her. Taking off his shirt, Mason enjoyed Lucy reach out for him and touch his defined chest.

"Hey, little lady. You're in Daddy's bedroom. I took you back to my house after you fell asleep in my arms on the car ride," Mason said, lifting her head and putting a pillow under it. Lucy watched as Mason slowly undressed her, biting her lip and not wanting to have sex at that moment.

"Daddy, I think we should wait. I'm not ready," Lucy said, trying to push his hands away. Mason just laughed and took off her headband.

"After everything, I've done for you today, do you really think Daddy is going to start being mean little one? I'm getting you ready for your bed, baby. I'm not going to fuck you just yet," Mason said, picking Lucy up, taking her by surprise.

"Aren't I heavy, Daddy," Lucy asked, feeling her bottom being rubbed by Mason's large hand as he carried her into his master bathroom.

"No, and even if you were, Daddy isn't going to miss an opportunity to feel all of this," Mason said, shaking Lucy's lingerie covered breasts on his bare chest. He carried her into the bathroom, kicking the double doors open and letting her take in the marble suite before gently placing her in the bathtub. It was warm, just as Mason had expected and watched as Lucy giggled, after being placed in there with her lingerie still on.

"Daddy, you are so silly, now I'm all wet," Lucy said, stretching out in the tub.

"Well, I wasn't sure if you were ready for Daddy to see you're big girl parts in person yet or not," Mason said, taking off his shoes, socks, and pants. He left on his briefs, happy that his semi-hard bulge made Lucy lick her lips involuntarily as he got into the tub with her.

"I'm ready," Lucy said, reaching around her back, wanting to take her bra off. Mason just smirked, reaching for her hands and unclipping the delicate lace garment, before moving his hands over her body and down to her panties.

"Then I guess these are coming off too," Mason said, pulling on her panties. He took Lucy's lingerie and placed it on the steps of the bath before going back to feel her body in his hands. Cupping her tits, he sighed as he felt her nipple piercings, the bars going through her nipples, making them hard and sensitive. Watching as Lucy moved against his touch, Mason felt his cock harden with excitement against briefs. Turning Lucy around, he pulled her into him and continued to play, stroking her soft, plump curves and enjoying their heavy weight. He knew Lucy could feel his cock against her as he pulled her on top of his lap, shuddering as her warm, soft thighs spread on his lap.

"Daddy, you're really big," Lucy said, reaching behind her and placing her hand on Mason's hard shaft. He smiled, reached into his briefs and pulled out his rod, letting Lucy feel it up her back as he reached around and stroked her pussy.

"Pretty shaven girl," Mason said, parting her lips with his finger and searching for her clit. Finding it, he stroked it, pushing Lucy back by her breast with one hand as his other toyed with her clit. Making circles around it, Lucy gasped as Mason pushed her hips forward slightly and repositioned his cock under her and along her slit.

"Sit on it, baby girl, let Daddy have your pussy lips either side of my cock," Mason whispered in her ear. Lucy could feel him pull at her puffy lips, making her sit on him, and her cunt hotdog his cock.

"I thought that would hurt," Lucy said, referring to her sitting on Mason's cock, as he began slowly sliding himself forward and back along her pussy. He just shook his head.

"I like it. I like to feel all of you," he replied, pulling harder on her tits. Lucy just moaned as he played, she had expected that he would simply stick himself inside of her, but this was different. It was sensual, the steam of the bath making the room foggy, the slow but deliberate strokes of his touch making her excited and wet. She had long forgotten that she didn't want to fuck him as he teased her, making her want to say yes to anything he requested.

"Will you let Daddy feel inside of you?" Mason asked, pushing Lucy's breasts together and rolling her nipples in his fingers.

"Yes, Daddy," Lucy said, feeling Mason lift her off him, just to hold her hips above his cock before slowly opening her with his tip.

"Oh, you are a tight little one," Mason said, feeling Lucy's pussy convulse around his head. Trying to enter her, Mason laughed as he was refused.

"You don't want Daddy inside of you just yet, is that it? Or are you just not used to having such a big dick want to explore you?" Mason asked, already knowing the answer.

"I've never had something so big before, Daddy. I do want you, I just don't think I can take you right now," Lucy said, feeling embarrassed she couldn't hold him inside of her. Mason just smirked and pulled out of Lucy, making her gasp as she felt the water around her stretched hole.

"That's ok, Daddy will open you up gently," Mason said, holding her naked body in his arms. Lucy snuggled into his neck, sitting on his lap and feeling his balls under her, his cock along her tummy.

"Don't fall asleep just yet little girl, Daddy still has to dress you for bed, come on, I better get you out of here before you fall asleep again," Mason said, standing up and taking a warm towel from the heated towel rack. He held Lucy's hand as he helped her from the bathtub, admiring her large perky breasts, little waist, and thick booty.

"How did Daddy get so lucky," Mason said as he felt Lucy up while he dried her. Giggling at his groping touch, Lucy wriggled in the towel as Mason dried her.

"Now now, young lady, don't try and get away from Daddy," he said, a slight warning in his voice as Lucy settled and let him explore her. Satisfied, Mason let the towel drop and took Lucy back into his room.

"Lay down over there," Mason instructed, pointing to a room. Lucy turned to see that he was pointing to a room which had a soft pink light coming from it. Naked, and slightly cold, Lucy walked into the room, shocked at what she saw. *This is what he was talking about,* Lucy said to herself, referring to the requirements of their contract. She remembered how Mason had said he wanted her as his baby girl that she would be diapered, bottle-fed and dressed like a baby.

"I said to lay down," Mason said, gently patting Lucy on her bottom, shaking her soft ass in his hand before pushing her forward. Lucy just remained speechless as she lay down on the changing table that was at the far side of the room.

"Good girl," Mason said, watching as Lucy took in the room. The walls were white with a feature wall of a jungle, with nocks and hooks on the trees to create an animal story. The thick charcoal carpet had a plush white rug in the middle of the room. An adult-sized, white crib was in the corner, and the changing table matched. A built-in cupboard had mirrored doors, and Lucy watched as inside those cupboards housed onesies hung up on wooden coathangers.

"Daddy is going to diaper you every night, little girl," Mason said, taking out a pink diaper and pacifier. Lucy saw that it was glittery and her eye grew big as Mason placed it in her mouth.

"That's a girl," he said, lifting her hips up and placing the diaper under her bottom. Lucy felt the cool powder tickle her as Mason rubbed it over the crease of her thighs meeting her pussy and before she realized it had happened, she was wearing a diaper.

"Don't you just look perfect," Mason said, shaking her breasts in both his hands. Lucy didn't know how to feel as he sat her up and took out one of the bra's he had bought her earlier that day and helped her put it on.

"Daddy will get you some bra's for sleeping in, but tonight you'll wear this," he said, pulling on the straps and admiring his sweet baby girl. He kissed the top of her head as he walked over to the cupboard and looked through the options.

"Hmm, which one," he said, looking back at Lucy who had moved to sit cross-legged on the table. Mason had bought new outfits after seeing Lucy's body on webcam and was happy he had done so. *God her tits are magnificent,* he thought selecting the pink love heart onesie with the deep V at the front to expose Lucy's generous cleavage.

"You are going to look so cute, little one," Mason said as a woman walked into the nursery.

"Will there be anything else for this evening, Sir?" She asked, looking at Lucy affectionately. Lucy just tried to hid her face as she burned red, having someone see her like this.

"No, that's everything, thanks, Ellen. Oh, Ellen, this is Lucy. Lucy, say hi to Ellen," Mason said, making Lucy's head spin.

"Hi, Ellen," she softly said, almost inaudibly. Ellen just smiled as she walked over to Lucy, who Mason was busy dressing.

"It's alright, little girl. I'm the housekeeper

here. You'll be seeing a lot of me. And I'll be seeing a lot of you in both big and little girl clothes. So you might as well get used to it, sweetheart," Ellen said. *She is not someone to mess around with;* Lucy thought as Ellen gave her a stern look. She was older than Mason and had the type of motherly figure with wide hips and enlarged breasts. *Probably brought on by hormones,* Lucy said to herself, getting lost in the way they pushed out against her uniform.

"I think she likes you, Ellen," Mason said, seeing how perplexed Lucy was on the older woman's breasts. Ellen just laughed, reaching out to stroke Lucy's soft cheek and hold her head to her breast gently.

"Well, so she should. She'll be on them soon enough," she said, holding Lucy still as she tried to wriggle away, alarmed at what she had just heard.

"That'll be everything, thank you, Ellen," Mason said with a loving smile, dismissing Ellen who kissed Lucy's cheek before dipping her head to Mason and leaving.

"Daddy, what does she mean?!" Lucy said in a frantic hiss, trying to be quiet but only amusing him.

"She runs this household, and she'll also be the one who looks after you when Daddy has to go on work trips or entertain clients during the evening. She's very good; you'll adore her. She's going to spoil you rotten; I can just see it," Mason said, opening one more clip on the front of Lucy's onesie and exposing the tops of her breasts to him. Picking her up and carrying her affectionately, Mason took her to the crib and placed her down gently.

"You're going to sleep here tonight, baby girl," he said, pulling the blankets back and tucking Lucy in. he took a thick fluffy pink blanket from the shelves in the cupboard as well as a selection of stuffies, unsure of which one Lucy would like.

"Daddy, are they all for me?" Lucy said, surprising herself that she fell into this dynamic with so much ease. Mason looked down at the collection he held in his arms as he thought for a moment.

"Yep," he said, deciding that Lucy could have whatever she wanted.

"I like spoiling you, little Lucy, make sure you don't become a little brat, or I'll take all your treats away, alright?" Mason said, dropping the toys on Lucy and making her giggle.

"Daddy!" Lucy said her little voice that she didn't know she had escaping and making Mason's eyes sparkle with affection.

"I won't Daddy; I don't want to make you mad," Lucy said, finding a fat purple kitty that she cuddled into, adjusting all the others around her.

"Goodnight, little one," Mason said, turning on the starry night light that decorated the high ceiling with multi-colored stars.

"Wow," Lucy said from behind her pacifier as her eyes danced across the ceiling, seeing how the stars faded and reappeared in another spot on the ceiling. Closing the door, quietly leaving the room, Mason smiled and looked up toward the ceiling in joy as he delighted in how their first meeting had gone.

Chapter 5

Lucy had faded off to sleep, feeling more relaxed than she had in a long time. The yearning for something she couldn't identify ceased to exist in Mason's arms, the pain she carried in her heart seemed to fade away.

Opening her eyes in the morning, Lucy heard Mason before she saw him.

"Yes, that will be fine. The timing is a little off; I have something I need to do here first. But I will be there by tomorrow," Mason said assertively. Lucy guessed he was just outside the closed door and wondered what the day would bring.

"Ellen, call Alfred. I need him tomorrow to take me to the airport. And tell Cherry that it will only take an hour and she will have him back," Mason said as he opened the door to the nursery.

"Well good morning baby girl," Mason said,

seeing that Lucy's big eyes with her long eyelashes were staring at him, smiling behind her pacifier.

"Daddy," Lucy said, lifting her arms to hug him as he stood outside her crib.

"Oh, what a sweet baby you are," Mason said, stroking her hair. He unlatched the railing and took down the slat spacing.

"Come to, Daddy, little one," Mason said, carrying Lucy out into the grand living room and placing her on the expensive chestnut leather couch. He set her up with her blankie and kitty before looking at his watch.

"Ellen," Mason called, hearing her quickening heavy footsteps. Lucy watched as Ellen walked into the room, seeing her properly for the first time. She had hazel eyes, lightly tanned skin, and a cheeky smile. Her hair was auburn and set in a fresh blowout with made Lucy wonder how beautiful she looked in her prime if she was this stunning now. *She's got to be like mid-forties,* Lucy thought to herself as Ellen's gaze landed upon her.

"Baby, Daddy has to run into town and pick

up the keys to a new property. I was meant to do it Monday, but something has come up, and I need to do it today. Also, I need to go away for a week tomorrow, unfortunately. I know we were going to spend the weekend together, but I now have to be there tomorrow sorry," Mason said, taking both of Lucy's hands in his and looking her in the eye.

"That's ok Daddy," Lucy said, trying not to sound disappointed.

"Good girl," Mason said. Before turning to Ellen.

"Has everything been set up as I asked?" He asked her who just nodded her head.

"Good," Mason said, turning back to Lucy.

"So, I've sorted out that roommate of yours, and you won't be sharing a room with her anymore. I have a feeling she would steal your things, and I can't have my little princess having her things taken," he said, making Lucy look at him curiously.

"Daddy, you didn't, kill her, did you?" Lucy said, genuinely, making Mason and Ellen laugh.

"No, baby girl. But I did have you moved into your own place. Don't worry. I've paid for it for the rest of the year so you can have your own space. Maybe after this year you come and live with Daddy, but I don't want to rush you. So you've got your own little apartment close to campus and a brand new bike and electric skateboard to get you there," Mason said, making Lucy's head spin.

"Daddy," was all Lucy could see. Seeing that he had made Lucy happy, Mason kissed her on both her cheeks before passing Ellen an envelope and walking out of the room to go and pack his bags.

"So, it'll just be you and me for the day little one. I'll drop you off into your new place in a little while and get you settled in," she said, making Lucy wonder what was in the envelope. Lucy looked up at the woman and wasn't really sure what she was meant to do next.

"Movie and breakfast?" Ellen suggested, laughing when Lucy gave her a toothy smile nodded her head, watching Ellen as she left the room. *What the fuck am I even doing,* Lucy thought, remembering the $15,000 shopping spree Mason had taken her on yesterday without even getting mad when she couldn't take him, how he had been so loving with her and looked after her in the evening.

"Um, Ellen, I have an assignment I really need to get done," Lucy said as Ellen came back into the room with a fruit platter.

"Then you better finish your fruit up little one; Aunty Ellen still has some milky's for you before I let you go," Ellen said, making Lucy's mind spin once again. As Lucy was rendered speechless, Ellen winked at her and fed Lucy a strawberry she willingly accepted.

"Come and cuddle up with Aunty Ellen," Ellen said, opening her arms to Lucy who moved over to cuddle her. Ellen's full breasts feeling like pillows against Lucy's cheek as the movie started. Ellen waited until Lucy's rigid body relaxed and began snuggling into her.

"Oh, you are a sweet little girl aren't you,"

Ellen said as Lucy sucked on her pacifier, making suckling sounds as she rested her hand on Ellen's breast.

"Sounds like you need a little bit more in your tummy," Ellen said, pulling out Lucy's pacifier and smirking at her pouty face.

"It's alright baby girl, Aunty Ellen will give you something else to put in that little mouth of yours," Ellen said, unbuttoning the front of her uniform and exposing her voluptuous breasts.

"I'm not into girls," Lucy suddenly nervously said.

"I'm not a girl, darling, I'm a woman. And I'm your Aunty so you'll be a good girl for me or you'll feel my punishment on your sweet little ass," Ellen said pulling the front of her bra down and resting her swollen breast on top.

"Don't fight me," Ellen said, putting Lucy into her arms, laying her on her back and rubbing her nipple on Lucy's lips.

"Open your mouth little girl," Ellen said, slapping Lucy's cheek swiftly as she denied her.

"Don't test me," Ellen said, warning in her voice as Lucy opened her lips.

"There's my good girl. Daddy will be so proud of you," Ellen said, sighing as she felt Lucy's lips tug on her milk filled breast. Suckling, Lucy closed her eyes as Ellen began humming her a tune, relaxing in her arms as Mason re-entered the room, leaning against the wall and smiling at the scene that played out in front of him.

"See you soon, little girl. Aunty Ellen will take care of you while Daddy is away. She's going to check on you every night, alright?" Mason said, holding Lucy's mouth to the older woman's breast when he saw her try to pull away from Ellen.

"Just nod if you understand little one, I don't want to tear you away," Mason said, watching as Lucy nodded her head. He kissed her goodbye and walked out of the room. Ellen continued to hold her as the movie ended and Lucy began playing instead of suckling.

"I think someone is full," Ellen said, pressing on Lucy's tummy and making her have to fight not to wet her diaper.

"Oh, didn't Daddy tell you, you'll wet your diaper before I let you get back into your big girl clothes," Ellen said to Lucy who just shook her head with Ellen's nipple still in her mouth.

"You can try and fight it. But that will only be painful for you, darling," Ellen said, placing her hand over Lucy's pussy, cupping her firmly. Lucy was surprised at the strength of the woman and wriggled in her arms, making Ellen smirk.

"Last chance," she warned, making Lucy whimper in reluctant obedience. Snuggling closer to Ellen, Lucy buried her face the woman's ample cleavage as she wet her diaper.

"Good girl," Ellen cooed, amused at Lucy's embarrassment. Continuing to hold her, Ellen patted Lucy's padded bottom and turned on the TV.

"I'm going to watch my show before I change you. So you remember to do what I ask you immediately, little one," Ellen said, putting her breast back into her bra and doing the buttons back up. Lucy sat on the couch, hating the feeling of the wet diaper against her skin and whined before Ellen bent her over her knee and gently patted her bottom for the two-hour-long special that played out on the enormous flat screen.

"Come on then. I think you've learned your lesson," Ellen said, rolling Lucy off her lap and watching as she fell on the floor.

"Silly girl, come here," Ellen said as Lucy stood and walked behind her. Ellen led her into another bathroom and gently undressed Lucy.

"Even when you are in your big girl clothes, you'll still call me Aunty Ellen, you do understand?" Ellen said to a nodding Lucy, who now stood naked in front of her. Ellen raised her eyebrow expectantly.

"Yes, Aunty Ellen," Lucy said making Ellen smile and walk away, taking Lucy's clothes and used diaper with her and disappearing as Lucy turned on the shower and let the water run over her body. *What the fuck, Lucy. What is this that you are getting yourself into?* Lucy thought as she let the raindrop feeling water pour down on her head. She had been in such shock by the way Mason had showered her in gifts, the kind of life she had spent years fantasizing over. She looked out of the shower and to her bag that had appeared on the elegant window seat in the bathroom and just smiled as she shook her head. *If all I have to do is fool around with these hot people and get all of this, that's something I can most certainly do,* Lucy decided in the quiet of her heart before turning the water off. Drying off and dressing in one of her new outfits, Lucy left the bathroom with her travel bag over her shoulder. Checking the pockets of the bag, she found her recently bought phone and tablet and smiled at how beautiful and shiny they looked.

"Oh, there you are. Ready to go?" Ellen said, coming out from behind what Lucy could only guess was her room. Why would Mason let the house staff live in his home? Lucy thought, dismissing her curiosity and nodding her head. She had hardly recognized Ellen as she stood before her in an outfit that made her look as though she was the one who lived the lavish lifestyle. She had that; *I come from generations of extreme wealth*, look about her with her elegance and way she carried herself to match.

"Right, let's go then," Ellen said, her high heels clicking through the house as she led Lucy to the garage.

"We are going in the Porsche, here, give me your bags," Ellen said, taking Lucy's bag off her shoulder and her handbag from her hands. Ellen smirked at how bewildered Lucy was as she looked around at the expensive exotic car collection Mason had acquired over the years.

"Buckle up sweetheart," Ellen said as Lucy sat in the front passenger seat and looked nervous. Quickly snapping into life, Lucy buckled her seatbelt and looked wide-eyed and vulnerable at Ellen.

"Where is my new apartment?" Lucy said in a soft voice, afraid that her life was being taken so far out of her own control.

"It's in one of the buildings Mason owns. It's close to your college; you're going to love it. I put a few of my own touches in as well. We organized it last night while you were asleep. You are lucky to have a Daddy like Mason sweetheart, he is gentle and loving, and there is nothing he can't give you," Ellen said, driving out of the grounds and onto the road. It felt as though Lucy had been living a dream, and within the last 24hours, everything she had ever wanted had become her reality. She looked out the window, letting Ellen's hand fall on her thigh and stroke her affectionately as she drove. Watching the tall trees of the picturesque street turn into the city, Lucy wondered how her new home would look. She was grateful for the first time in years that her real family didn't seem too worried about what she did or didn't do, having been quite blunt in their reaction when she told them she had been accepted into college. They had assumed she would live their life. The life where she had a job at a store and married young, having a few kids who went to the local school and having to find ways to cut costs so they would make ends meat. But that wasn't what she wanted at all. She wanted more; she demanded more. Not from anyone in particular, but from herself. She knew that if she could be college-educated, she would have a better life, and as she saw the building, Ellen was driving her into the garage too, she knew she had been right in some respect.

"Home sweet home, baby girl," Ellen said, parking and getting out of the car. She popped the trunk, got Lucy's bags, and began walking to the elevator, Lucy in tow.

"You'll need these," Ellen said, handing Lucy a key card that she assumed opened the door to the apartment. The elevator chimed and came to a stop, opening its doors and leaving Lucy speechless. There was only one other apartment on this level, and as Ellen opened the door with her own card, Lucy just shook her head in disbelief.

"What, the actual, fuck!?" Lucy said, walking in circles around the entrance of the penthouse suite.

"Now now, no need for bad language, young lady," Ellen said, causing Lucy to bring her hands over her mouth. She ran to the floor to ceiling, wall-length window and looked out over the city, over the park and lake and could see the flags of her college.

"So, here is everything you need to know about how to operate your new home," Ellen said, showing Lucy a black leather folder on the coffee table.

"And, the fridge and pantry are already stocked. While Mason is away, I will come over every night to get you ready for bed, and every morning to get you ready for your day. Also, I have a card, so does Mason, so if you come home and we are here, don't be surprised. I think that's everything. Oh, one last thing. Everything that you two bought yesterday, is already here, plus a few little treats I got you because I know you didn't have time to buy any jewelry yesterday and well, that simply will not do. You can't be walking around without at least this," Ellen said, taking out a bracelet of diamonds and rose gold and securing it around Lucy's wrist.

"There, perfect," Ellen said, pulling Lucy in and holding her lovingly before kissing her cheek and walking towards the door.

"See you tonight, darling," Ellen said, smirking at Lucy's still shocked expression before closing the front door behind herself.

Lucy just stayed standing where she was and shook her head, trying to understand what had just happened. *He must really like me,* she thought, going to the fridge and seeing that there were fruits and vegetables, dips and meals all labeled with the packaging of expensive restaurants and delis. She took out a bottle of flavored water and sat down on the couch as Mason text her.

Hi sweet girl, I hope everything is to your liking. I've left a timetable for you to fill out on the kitchen bench so I know when it's best to talk with you. Can you fill it in and message it to me? I know you have the assignment you need to get done, finish that today so I can talk to you tonight. Love Daddy x

Lucy got up and walked to the kitchen and looked at the timetable, taking the pen that laid next to it and began filling it out. Sending Mason a photo of her weekly schedule, she wondered if he wanted more. So sending him a photo of her laying on top of the bed in her new bedroom, she wrote.

I can't wait to show you how grateful I am for everything you've done for me, Daddy. Love, your baby girl XX

Mason looked at the photo she had sent and smirked, knowing that she didn't have time to be naughty, he wanted that paper finished.

You're a sweet little tease. But Daddy wants that paper done today. So get busy little girl, I expect perfect grades from you X

Lucy smiled as she put her phone away and went to get her laptop, opening it up and continued to write her essay.

Chapter 6

Mason had been away for the following week just as he had said, with Ellen coming to the apartment every day at 5 pm and staying until 11 pm, just to return at 7 am and stay after Lucy had left for college. Ellen, being true to her word, had regressed Lucy every night, only to trigger her back into being an adult during their mornings together. Mason had video chatted with the both of them every night, enjoying how Ellen mothered Lucy but sending Lucy dirty messages throughout the day until the afternoon.

Yeah, you love it when Daddy sauce squirts into your mouth. Oh, good girl, drink up that protein shake, let Daddy pour it down your throat. It's thick isn't it baby girl. Swallow it all up; Daddy isn't finished with you yet, then you can get your teddy when I am done. You are going to let Daddy take a photo of that cream oozing from your lips, Mason wrote.

Lucy had been sitting in the back row of the lecture theatre so nobody could look over her shoulder at the filthy messages that flooded her phone. Smiling as she wrote back, wanting to match Mason's efforts to make her cum just by reading his texts.

I'd love to feel you cuff my wrists behind my back, Daddy, and make me sit on your lap, your cock spearing my pussy open as your balls slapped against my asshole with each bounce you forced me to take. I'm going to be such a good girl for you and show you my pretty pink pussy, let you fill my tight cunt with your big cock until I have to gasp as it fills me. Mason saw that message as he walked down a corridor and around the corner, breathing deeply as he walked fast as to keep his cock from going hard.

Are you in your lecture now, baby girl? I hope you aren't wearing any panties like you are supposed to. Go sit in the front of the class, spread your thighs and let your lecturer see your pretty pussy. Mason wrote, making Lucy frown. He hadn't said anything about sharing her with another man before, even if her professor wasn't there yet, she knew that within 2 minutes he would be and would have a clear view of Lucy's most private place. Reluctantly, Lucy collected her things and made her way down to the front of the class. Happy that no one ever sat at the front, she spread her thighs, feeling the aircon on her clit and waited for her seedy professor to come in.

Well, aren't you a good girl, Mason messaged next before walking through the glass door of the lecture theatre and looking directly at Lucy who just stared at him with shock. He winked at her, unnoticed by the other students who continued to talk or look through their phones and laptops. Giving a sly smirk, Lucy took her laptop out and pushed her hips forward, giving Mason a better view of her.

"Hello, all you wannabees. How are you today?" Mason said, making Lucy laugh and the lecture theatre go quiet.

"I say wannabees because up until now you have not had me, and therefore, have been gravely uneducated. But have no fear, Daddy's here now, and I am going to make you great," Mason said making the students laugh.

The lecture continued, with the slutty girls of the course fawning over him and the boys wishing they had the expensive toys Mason had. Lucy's degree was in business and commerce, and the unit Mason was now in charge of was in marketing, or how he liked to call it, 'How to get people to give you their money.' Lucy watched as he dazzled the students for the two-hour lecture, taking more notes than she had ever done in her life. As the lecture came to an end, the students cleared out of the theatre, but Lucy stayed, surprised at how her life was turning out.

"You're Lucy, right?" Mason said playfully as Lucy jumped up from her seat and hugged him tightly.

"I know sweetheart, but we can't do that

here. How about I meet you back at yours in about an hour? Daddy wants to see how that little pussy opens up for me," Mason said softly before turning and walking out of the theatre. Lucy walked the other direction, practically ran for her bike and pedaled home as fast as she could.

"Woah, easy there," Ellen said, as Lucy rushed through the front door.

"What? It's only 3 pm, what are you doing here?" Lucy said, surprised to see Ellen. Ellen just raised an eyebrow, swiftly grabbed Lucy by her wrist and pulled her into her, spanking Lucy's bottom quickly and making her double over to try and escape.

"I'm sorry, I'm sorry, Aunty Ellen," Lucy wailed as Ellen belted her bottom with her hand.

"You will be sorry," Ellen said, pulling up Lucy's skirt to see her red handprints on Lucy's skin. Spanking her several more times until Lucy became limp in her arms, Ellen stopped and held Lucy's chin in her hand, looking at her expectantly.

"I really am sorry, Aunty Ellen," Lucy said. Satisfied as a tear rolled down Lucy's cheek, Ellen let her go and returned to her usual loving self.

"I have put new flowers in the bathroom, and your room, baby girl," Ellen said, as Mason walked through the front door.

"Oh, my favorite girls," he said, copping an eye roll from Ellen who dipped her head to Mason and went to sit on the couch and read a book.

"Daddy!" Lucy said, lifting her arms and jumping into his arms, getting cuddled close as Mason gave her kisses all over her face.

"Ellen, I'm going to go fuck this pretty girl," Mason said, carrying Lucy into her bedroom and kicking the door shut behind him. He walked Lucy over to the bed, kissing her passionately on the mouth, exploring her with his tongue and groaning into her mouth.

"God, you taste sweet," he said, dropping her onto the bed.

"Take your skirt off for Daddy," he instructed, crossing his arms across his chest and watching her expectantly. Lucy just giggled and got to her knees, reaching around the back of her skirt and slowly unzipping it. Wriggling her hips, Mason loved how the material got caught on her ample booty and reached forward to help her take it off.

"I can't wait to bury my cock in here," he said almost to himself as he reached between her thighs and stroked her slit, licking his lips when he felt how wet she was.

"Yeah, that's what Daddy likes," he said, pulling on her singlet off with his free hand. Lucy just moaned as he toyed with her, rubbing over her clit, and feeling her softness against his rough hand.

"Shake your titties for Daddy," Mason instructed, watching how Lucy's breasts swayed from side to side in her Chanel bra.

"Bounce them," he said, enjoying how they shook.

"Does it hurt, having these big titties shake for Daddy?" Mason asked, seeing Lucy wince slightly as they dropped with each bounce she did for him.

"A little bit Daddy," Lucy said, feeling Mason push her pussy lips back and slide his finger into her.

"That's ok; you'll learn to love being in pain for Daddy. Just say red like we talked about if it gets too much, but you can take a little pain can't you baby girl," Mason said reaching out and pulling her tits out of her bra and flicking her nipples.

"Such a dirty girl," Mason said as he toyed with her, sticking another finger into her pussy and wiggling his fingers over her G-spot.

"Oh, there is it," he said, watching how Lucy's eyes rolled back and her pussy became wetter.

"Juicy little girl," Mason said, watching as Lucy's hips took over and she began to grind down on his hand. Mason had felt his cock get increasingly hard as he played with Lucy and took her hands to unzip his pants.

"You know what to do," he said, taking her chin in his hand and making her look at him as she felt his cock spring from his pants, his belt buckle hanging from his trousers as she began to give him a handjob with both her hands.

"Can you feel how much I want you?" Mason said, pushing himself into Lucy's hands and letting her chin go.

"Put Daddy in your mouth," Mason said, pushing Lucy's head down onto his waiting rod. Sliding into her throat, Mason was pleasantly surprised how she took him, gagging around his shaft as he filled her mouth.

"Oh, I love that you are just as much of a slut as you said you were. Daddy doesn't like liars," Mason said, pulling out of her pussy slowly as his cock also exited her mouth.

"Lay down," Mason said, positioning himself above her. He slowly stroked his cock, jerking the cum from his shaft and letting it spurt onto Lucy's tummy.

"Let's see," he added, putting the tip of his

rock hard cut cock into her.

"Yeah baby girl," Mason said feeling how easily she took him, pushing into her with more intensity and grinning as she gasped for air as his locked his hips down on hers and filled her.

"It feels so good to have you finally," Mason said, keeping his cock inside of Lucy as he kissed her forehead and stroked her hair. He waited until Lucy's muscles relaxed around him, but enjoying how her cunt squeezed him.

"You are a sweet little baby girl, aren't you, Lucy?" Mason said, pulling out of her just to push back in, getting squeezed all over again.

"I'm going to destroy that pretty little cunt," Mason said, holding Lucy's face in both his hands as he began to pound her, kissing her as she moaned. Mason didn't have to wait very long to feel Lucy's cum coat his cock as he pumped her.

"That's it, take Daddy's cock like a good girl," Mason said as he held his hand to her throat and choked her as he came his cum wetting the bed cover as he continued to plow Lucy, groaning as he emptied himself inside of her. Slapping the side of Lucy's thigh as he pulled out of her, Mason looked down at the beautiful girl who willingly gave herself to him and smiled.

"Ellen, come and help my little girl get clean and ready to be my baby girl," Mason yelled, as he bent down to kiss Lucy's forehead before disappearing into the bathroom. Lucy waited for Ellen to come into the room, and she tried to cover herself, which just made Ellen laugh.

"Not much point of that, I've seen your little body all week, haven't I. Did Daddy play his grown-up games with you, baby girl? Are you ready to be little again?" Ellen said, taking Lucy's hand and standing her up, noticing how Lucy doubled forward and held her pelvis.

"Did Daddy hurt you with his big cock? Let's get you in a nice relaxing bath sweet girl," Ellen said, gently reaching around Lucy's smaller body and walking her to the second bathroom and sitting her in the tub. Ellen took the unicorn bubble bath and made the room smell like strawberries as the warm water mixed with the bubbles. She put Lucy's pacifier in her mouth and watched as Lucy didn't try to fight her for the first time all week. Noticing how easily and willingly Lucy regressed, Ellen sat by the bath and tenderly washed Lucy's body with a washcloth.

"We will get you all snuggly, and you can cuddle up with Daddy on the couch, alright?" Ellen said, as Lucy nodded but reached for her.

"You are going to get me wet too, little girl," Ellen said, taking Lucy's arms and putting them back down into the bath. Lucy just pouted, her big wide, innocent eyes softening Ellen's heart.

"Out you come," she finally said, feeling the water turning cold. Lucy noticed how she didn't feel so sensitive anymore and stood still as Ellen dried her, giggling as Mason walked into the room.

"Thanks, Ellen," he said, taking over and putting the towel back on the heated towel rack and taking Lucy's hand, walking her back into her room.

"Daddy, we do it over here," Lucy said from

behind her pacifier making Mason laugh.

"Alright sweetie," he said, taking the diaper, Ellen passed him before walking out of the room. Diapering Lucy, Mason dressed her in a pink and black cheater print diaper cover, and black lace Fendi bra, her tight black long sleeve pull-over, over the top.

"Which sockies do you want darling?" Mason said, watching how Lucy crawled over to the cupboard which contained all her baby things. Lucy sat and looked up, trying to decide.

"What do you think?" Mason said, sitting down beside Lucy and making her snuggle into him.

"These ones, Daddy," Lucy said, frowning when Mason shook his head.

"Please, Daddy," he corrected gently.

"Please, Daddy," Lucy said, blushing slightly that she hadn't used her manners. Smiling, Mason stood back up and took down the fluffy pink socks Lucy had selected and rolled them up her cold legs.

"Oh sweetie, let's get you wrapped in a

blankie with something yummy and warm to eat," Mason said, walking into the kitchen, followed by Lucy who crawled after him.

"What's for dinner, Ellen?" Mason said, making her raise her head questioningly.

"Well, you're back now, how about you organize it?" She said a smirk on her face.

"Oh, because you just make everything taste so much better than I can. Please, Ellen?" Mason said playfully, picking Lucy up and putting her into Ellen's arms. Holding the young girl to her with loving affection, Ellen rolled her eyes and tenderly reached out to rub Mason's cheek.

"I'm so good to you," Ellen said, kissing Lucy before settling her on the couch with the blankie Mason handed her. Ellen turned on the tv above the roaring fireplace before getting up and walking to the kitchen.

"What would I do without you?" Mason called as Lucy rested her head on his lap. Ellen just mumbled something under her breath as she got dinner ready, enjoying the scene that played out in front of her. Lucy regressed and deep in her little space, Mason watching the football while carelessly patting Lucy until she was almost asleep. Ellen banged a few pots together, waking Lucy up and smirked before going back to cooking.

"Daddy, where did you meet Aunty Ellen?" Lucy said, surprised that Mason's life was nothing like anything she thought could ever exist. Mason just smirked as wondered how to answer her question.

"The same place I met Alfred, the man who drove us around town on our first date," he replied, stopping as Ellen placed dinner on the elegant dining table.

"Up you come," Mason said, picking Lucy up and carrying her to the dining room. Placing her down, she was excited to see her creamy pumpkin soup in her tiger bowl. Her sippy cup next to it filled with a chocolate protein shake and her spoon by Mason's bowl.

"Let Daddy feed you," Mason said as Lucy reached for the spoon. Lucy felt Ellen drape a pink bib around her neck and clip it up behind her, bending down to kiss her cheek before going to sit down. Mason sipped his beer and sighing as though all the stresses of the day had magically disappeared before taking Lucy's spoon and feeding her, making sure the soup wasn't too hot.

"I'm so happy I could be home for dinner tonight," Mason said, eating his own soup hungrily, receiving more when he had almost finished his bowl.

"Ellen, thank you for looking after my little one while I was away, I hope she wasn't any trouble," Mason said, putting Lucy's paci back in her mouth as she had finished her dinner.

"She was surprisingly good. You got lucky with this little one," Ellen said, getting up to tidy the dishes away. Mason stayed sitting at the table, another beer in his hand as he watched Lucy crawl around the living room floor. She played with her blocks and stuffies, making homes for them and creating stories she then drew about with her crayons.

"I don't think life gets any better than this," Mason said as Ellen came back from putting everything in the dishwasher and turning it on. She had bought a glass of Sherry to the table and sipped it as she too watched Lucy.

"No, I don't think it really does," she said sipping as the fire warmed the room, moving over to the couch and placing a faux fur blanket over her knees as she read her book and Mason listened to an audiobook on real estate buying.

Chapter 7

"Lucy, Daddy's home," Mason called as he entered her apartment. He knew he was early and that she wouldn't be home yet but enjoyed calling out anyway.

"You know she isn't here," Ellen said, surprising Mason when she walked out from Lucy's bedroom after making the bed.

"Oh, what are you doing here?" Mason asked, putting his hands on his hips and looking at her for an explanation.

"I'm working. Your little one can't make a bed to save herself," Ellen said, walking past him and into the kitchen. She turned the kettle on, looking back to Mason who just nodded his head.

"Get me the tea then, it's in the cupboard," Ellen instructed, watching as Mason followed her order.

"Sit down; I need to run through the

expenses with you," Ellen said, taking two mugs down from the shelf. She put the tea into the teapot and poured in hot water before placing it on a tray along with the two mugs and carried it over to the table.

"This right here. She's doing it again," Ellen said, opening her laptop and showing him the peak in spending.

"You have to cut her loose. Don't give me your sad sop story about how she needs you; she obviously doesn't. You are just lucky Lucy is so sweet and clueless," Ellen continued

"She's only doing it because she saw me with Lucy on our first date. She's just having a tantrum. This is nothing to worry about," Mason replied, sipping the tea. Ellen just looked at him like he had lost his mind.

"What? She is fun, anyway. She wasn't even meant to be working that day, she must have switched shifts or something," Mason continued, ignoring the looks Ellen gave him.

"We have worked too hard for too long to

have that stupid little bitch run us into the ground," Ellen hissed, her eyes now burning holes in Mason. He just sighed an irritated sigh.

"I am aware of how hard we have worked," Mason said, trying to reach for Ellen's hand, only to have her pull away from him.

"Is this because Ella never let you mother her, but Lucy does?" Mason questioned, mischief in his voice. Ellen just rolled her eyes dramatically and scoffed.

"No. It has to do with you bringing a new girl home, regressing her and then leaving her because your spoilt brat called for her Daddy," Ellen said, hurting Mason with her direct manner.

"Ella has been nothing but trouble the minute you showed her the slightest of interests, and I know that thrills you, but Lucy deserves better, and you know it," Ellen said getting up just as Lucy opened the door to the apartment.

"Hi, sweetie," Ellen said, embracing her and kissing her on the cheek.

"Are you going already, Aunty Ellen?" Lucy

asked, snuggling into her affectionately. Lucy loved Ellen's sensual smelling perfume and had fallen asleep with it filling her senses on more than one occasion.

"I need to darling; I have some things to take care of," Ellen said, eyeing Mason who just rolled his eyes. Ellen kissed Lucy again before walking out of the apartment and closing the door behind her.

"Don't mind her, she is just a grump," Mason said, coming over and lifting Lucy into his arms.

"Baby girl, how come you never spend Daddy's money or ask if I can get you something else?" Mason asked, catching Lucy off guard.

"What do you mean? You give me my allowance, should I ask for more?" Lucy asked, shocked that he would ask such a question.

"Well, no, I guess not. Why aren't you a brat?" Mason questioned, not understanding why one girl would have a $12,000 shopping spree during her tantrum and the other happy to be given whatever he suited giving her.

"Daddy. I don't understand. Look at everything you have given me! I am so grateful, that's why I'm not a brat," Lucy said, coming to sit next to him. Mason thought deeply as he opened his arms and held Lucy.

"You are the perfect baby, do you know that?" Mason said, taking out his wallet and putting a couple of hundred dollars on the coffee table.

"Tomorrow, go get yourself something nice. You deserve to celebrate," he added, confusing Lucy.

"What am I celebrating?" Lucy questioned.

"The top grade that you got on your paper," Mason said, running his hands over her breasts as he spoke.

"Don't look at me like that. I had your essay cross graded so that no one could ever say it's because you are my sweet and beautiful little one that you got such a grade," Mason said, having his hands slapped away and given a disbelieving look.

"Wow, really," Lucy said, getting lost in her happiness of having succeeded in something she had been working so hard on but not having truly believed she could achieve.

"Yes, so let Daddy have these back, they are like big stress balls. One touch and I'm instantly more relaxed," Mason said, unbuttoning Lucy's blouse and opening it, revealing her ample breasts.

"Oh, is this new?" Mason said, admiring the soft pink lace push-up bra Lucy was wearing.

"Yes, Daddy," Lucy said, reaching around to unclip it. Mason just took her hands away and admired her soft, womanly body. Taking in her form and the gentle creases of her tummy before kissing her passionately.

"Daddy," Lucy giggled, only arousing him further. He lay her down on the couch, loosening his tie and taking off his blue business shirt. Lucy felt his muscled chest and laughed when he wiggled his hips on top of her.

"Lift your skirt up," Mason instructed, watching as Lucy obeyed.

"Show Daddy," he continued, leaning back off her and looking at her naked pussy. He grinned as she opened her cunt for him and watched as she pulled his rod from his pants, surprised it was already hard.

"Stay like that," Mason said, getting off her and disappearing into the bedroom. Coming back, Lucy saw he carried a tube of lube and a pair of nipple clamps.

"Daddy," Lucy said, resting on her elbows, only to be pushed back down by Mason.

"You don't have to be scared, little one; Daddy wouldn't hurt his baby girl," Mason said, lubing Lucy's pussy before rubbing his wet fingers over his shaft.

"Good girl," Mason said, entering Lucy slowly, feeling her accept him.

"Oh god yeah, baby!" Mason exclaimed hitting her hilt in one slow motion, feeling his balls be squeezed between him and Lucy.

"Oh just let me enjoy this for a minute," Mason said a she felt Lucy wiggle, wanting him out of her as she was stretched. Mason kept his cock stuffing Lucy's tight cunt as he pinched her nipples through her bra and clamped the metal objects to her, flicking them and making her pussy relax as her attention went to her breasts.

"That's it," Mason said, pulling out just to push back in it.

"That's sexy," Mason said, placing his hands on either side of Lucy, he pounded her, watching as the clamps shook with each thrust and ragged breath Lucy took. Reaching for Lucy's clit, Mason smirked as he felt her buck her hips, wanting him to give her the release she so desperately craved.

"Not yet," Mason playfully teased as he rubbed her clit faster, wondering how much she could take before she came against his cock. Lucy felt Mason's hands on her wrists as he thrust deeper and harder into her, kissing her as she moaned.

"You can cum now baby," Mason said, not having to repeat himself as Lucy squirted, exciting Mason who fucked her more vigorously.

"Did you like that baby?" Mason said, pumping her, wanting to shoot his load up her. Lucy just nodded her head as Mason removed his hands from Lucy's wrists and gripped her breasts, shaking them and using them to steady himself as he continued to drill Lucy's wet pussy.

"Daddy's got you," Mason said as he heard Lucy whimper just as he exploded inside her.

"Damn baby," Mason groaned as he felt a shiver go through his body, creaming inside of Lucy again. Pulling out, Mason sat back on the couch and breathed deeply as he closed his eyes and rested his head on the back on the couch.

"Get down here," he instructed, feeling Lucy's mouth on his cock, licking and kissing him.

"Suck it," he said, opening his eyes and looking down, reaching for her tits and laughing as Lucy gagged on his cock.

"My dick looks good in your mouth; I should have had you sucking me off long ago," Mason said, placing his hand on the back of her head and fucking her face until she was gasping for air.

"Swallow that all up baby girl," Mason said, watching as Lucy swallowed the cream he had just pumped into her mouth. Pulling his cock out of her mouth, he laughed as she dribbled her spit and his cum onto the top of her titties, making him reach down and push them together.

"Hold your titties together like that, yeah," Mason said, watching as Lucy shook the clamps as she obeyed him.

"Spit into that deep slit," Mason said, smiling as Lucy followed his orders. Spitting onto his cock, Mason bent his knees as he began titty fucking Lucy.

"Bend your head and stick your tongue out," he ordered, getting his tip licked with each trust forward.

"Oh, you are a good girl for Daddy," Mason groaned, as he came over her tongue, making it slip off her lips and onto her tits. He finished by grabbing the back of her head and cumming over the top of her titties.

"Yeah, you've got those porn star titties baby girl," Mason said, pulling her hands away and enjoying the mess he had made of her.

"Shake those big ol' titties for Daddy," Mason said, watching as Lucy began shaking them from side to side.

"Yeah that's good," Mason said, moving behind Lucy and trying to push his cock back into her pussy, laughing when she took him quickly, bending forward and pushing herself down on him.

"You need a good fuck before you be Daddy's little slut don't you," Mason said, as he began fucking her roughly.

"Yes, Daddy," Lucy moaned as Mason grabbed her hair and pushed her forward, came quickly, laughing and pulling out of her again.

"Let's get you showered," he said, standing back up and watching as Lucy stayed sitting on the floor.

"But Daddy," Lucy said, reaching down to play with her cunt.

"No baby girl. That's all you're getting tonight. Let Daddy make you his little baby girl now," Mason said, making Lucy roll her eyes and groan in frustration.

"Oh, does someone want to make Daddy mad?" Mason said, laughing at Lucy who quickly jumped to her feet and walked to where Mason was standing. Copping a hard slap on her ass as she passed him and walked into the bathroom.

"Oh, you get started, have a shower. Daddy needs to take this," Mason said, hearing his phone ring. Walking back out to the living room, Mason saw Ella's number on his phone.

"Hi," he said, hearing the water of the shower start, he walked into the laundry and shut the door.

"Daddy, why don't you come over. I need you; I hurt myself," Ella said down the phone, making Mason instantly worried.

"What do you mean you've hurt yourself?" He asked.

"I was getting a drink of water, and the

glass slipped from my hands, and I've got cuts everywhere, and there's so much blood," Ella replied, holding her breath.

"Alright, Daddy is on his way. Give me 30 minutes," Mason replied as he ended the conversation. Going back into the bathroom, Mason got into the shower with Lucy who was already clean.

"Baby girl, I have to go," Mason said making Lucy pout but nod her head.

"Work?" Lucy asked. Mason just grimaced and nodded as he quickly washed himself.

"Yeah, baby. Do you want me to get Ellen over here?" Mason said, but Lucy was already shaking her head no.

"I have a few things I need to do anyway," she said, getting a kiss on her forehead and watched as Mason left the bathroom.

Chapter 8

Lucy spent the night looking through social media and eating her weight in junk food. When she had told Mason she had things to do; she had lied. Instead, she had spent the evening tracking him. With all the dirty talk, expensive gifts and learning about a kink she had no idea she loved so much, Mason had never once asked about her. What her dreams were, what her skills were, or even just what she liked. He had no idea she could hack a computer or stick a tracer to his jacket under the collar so he wouldn't find it. He had no understanding that she outsourced her college essays and that he was just one of three other Daddy's who now funded her lifestyle. And with all of the things Mason didn't know about her, the one thing he hadn't learned was that Lucy knew the devil is in the detail. Mason had told her that he was in the real estate business, and yet, when she had gone through his emails and hidden files and checked them against the real estate deals, he had apparently made, his name wasn't on any of it. Ellen's was. So was Alfred's, Cherry's, and a woman named Ella S. But this wasn't the only thing that Mason seemed to avoid having his name on. There were no bank account records in his name. No companies, no shares or stocks. Nothing. Everything was in those four other names. *So, where does all your money come from*, Lucy thought to herself as she began tracking Ellen's accounts.

It was past midnight when Lucy heard her front door open, waking her up and making her realize that she had fallen asleep. Quickly tiding her printed papers and laptop away, Lucy rubbed her eyes as the living room light was turned on.

"Oh my god. I thought you'd be tucked up in bed," Ellen said, holding her hand to her chest, clearly taken aback by Lucy's presence.

"Sorry Aunty Ellen, but Daddy had to work, so I just stayed up doing my assignment," Lucy said, making Ellen frown.

"What do you mean he had to work?" Ellen said, coming to sit down on the couch next to Lucy.

"We fooled around, had a shower, then he got a phone call and said he had to go to work," Lucy said shrugging her shoulders, somewhat aware that work didn't really mean work. Ellen just angrily sucked in her cheeks before getting up to make a pot of tea. Offering Lucy a mug, Lucy just nodded her head before getting up to put her work in her bedroom. Coming back out into the living room, she sat down next to Ellen and looked her dead in the eye.

"He is seeing someone else isn't he," Lucy asked Ellen who maintained her composure as she tried to think of how to respond.

"No sweetie. He has international clients. So when it's night here, it's the day there. That's why he works such bizarre hours," Ellen replied, reaching out to tuck Lucy's hair behind her ear. Lucy wondered what the relationship between Mason and the older woman was. She wasn't his mother; Lucy was sure of that. But there was something there. She didn't simply work for him, and she knew Ellen knew exactly were Mason was at that very moment. She also wondered what her role was in the whole thing.

"Let's ring him, shall we? He will be at the office," Ellen suggested, pulling out her phone and finding Mason's number, ringing him before Lucy could form a rebuttal.

"Hi there, Lucy is just wondering when you'll be finished work for the evening. She misses her Daddy," Ellen said, smirking at Lucy who tried to keep up the game she was playing. Ellen nodded her head before speaking again.

"Well, you better finish what you started, because today is a new day and I'd hate to see little Lucy upset for much longer," Ellen said, ending the conversation with a click of her finger.

"He has to stay at the office tonight. Something about tying up some loose ends. He will be all yours by morning," Ellen said, pulling Lucy into her and holding her gently as Lucy fell asleep against her breasts.

Mason had been distant with Lucy for the rest of the week. Sure they had fucked, he regressed her, and they had gone shopping again, but he hadn't been into it. In fact, Lucy was wondering what she could do to excite him and have his attention back on her when it was clearly somewhere else. Ellen had said that it was just because he had been busy at work, but Lucy hadn't seen him at college all week.

"Daddy, how about we do something crazy?" Lucy suggested as they ate breakfast at an expensive restaurant on Saturday morning. Mason looked up from his tablet and raised an eyebrow at her.

"Let's go shooting," Lucy said, making Mason laugh.

"Shooting?" He questioned, receiving a very excited nodding from Lucy.

"We could play dress ups, and you could teach me how to shoot. There's a range right around the corner from here," Lucy explained gaining Mason's interest for the first time all week.

"Now what makes you think I know how to shoot?" He asked, giving her a curious expression. Lucy just shrugged her shoulders.

"You're good at everything else, I just assume you can do this too," Lucy said honestly. The waitress came to their table to take away their plates, and Mason waited until she was gone before speaking again.

"Well, when you put it that way," he said, his cheeky grin coming back on his handsome face as he got up and helped Lucy from her chair, taking her hand and leaving.

"You have to hold it like this," Mason said coming behind Lucy and doing all the typical boy teaches girl moves. He liked feeling like he was giving Lucy something she hadn't had before and helped her shoot before going to his own rifle and letting off a couple of rounds.

"Woah. This is just what I needed baby girl,

thank you," Mason said, lifting up her earmuffs and kissing her cheek. Lucy watched how he emptied the rounds with expert precision. *I thought so,* Lucy thought to herself. She had guessed that Mason had been given some form of formal training and this proved it. He hadn't seen her looking at him as he reloaded without looking at the rifle and began shooting again. *It can't be military; it's something darker,* she thought, coming to stand behind him and wrapping her arms around his waist lovingly. Mason finished the magazine and placed his rifle down, looking down at Lucy and beaming at her.

"You are awesome," he said, holding her affectionately for the first time all week.

"What do you want to do now?" He asked, pouting slightly when Lucy yawned and said she wanted to go back home for a nap.

"You've worn me out, Daddy," Lucy said quietly in his ear. Walking out of the range, Mason and Lucy waited for Alfred to pick them up.

"Do you have to work late tonight, Daddy?"

Lucy said, snuggling into him as Alfred pulled up. Opening her door, Mason put Lucy into the back seat as he walked around to jump into the front.

"Riding up here today, Sir?" Alfred asked Mason curiously.

"Yeah, I feel like a change from the back, and Lucy said she was tired so now she can lay down and rest on the way back to her apartment," Mason said. Alfred just nodded as he made a U-turn and began to drive to Lucy's house. Lucy was curious. She took out the recording device from her handbag and placed it in the back of the car, taking the other one out as it had run out of battery. Arriving at her apartment, Lucy got out of the car, kissed Mason goodbye and put her earphones in as the app on her phone activated the recording.

"Sir, we have a problem with the Italians," Lucy heard Alfred say, making her nod her head with the confirmation that something wasn't right about Mason.

"I don't know why. They got what they paid

for. If they wanted something extra, that'd have to be another conversation," Mason replied.

"Jimmy, they said they aren't going to wait much longer, you have to meet with the Irish and tell them that they'll have to wait. We need the Italians right now," Alfred said. *Who is Jimmy?* Lucy thought, her eyes going wide when she heard Mason speak again.

"Don't call me that. My name is Mason, Mason Carter. That's who you lot made me. Jimmy is just some street rat who caught a lucky break," Mason said aggressively.

"And don't worry about the Irish. As long as I've got my dick in their pretty little princess Ella, they'll do what I say," Mason said, laughing to himself.

"Also, Ellen wants to know what your plans are with Lucy," Alfred continued, making Lucy interested in his plans for her as well.

"Oh, not you too," Mason groaned.

"Look. Lucy is separate to all of this. She is beautiful, young, and pure. She is the one thing that makes all this shit worthwhile, and I am not getting rid of her just because a couple of gangsters are having an argument. I'll get the guns to the Italians. I'll get the gear to the Irish. And I'll get the cash to the politicians, alright. I haven't let you lot down yet have I?" Mason snarled, making Lucy smile that he thought so highly of her. *So, he's a freelancer;* she thought to herself walking into her apartment, closing the door behind her and leaning against the door. *Ella?* Lucy suddenly thought, wondering if it was the same Ella who she used to share a dorm room.

Chapter 9

"You are awfully quiet today," Mason said as they walked through the park the following week. This had become their favorite spot. Down by the water, the boats sailing in the out on the open sea, people are flying kites up the banks. Here the world seemed simpler. *That's probably why I love it; I don't have to be worried the man I'm sleeping with is the crime lord of the burrow,* Lucy thought as Mason took her hand in his.

"I've just got a lot of work to do. It's almost the end of the semester; there's all there are exams and essays. Honestly, I'm not sure if I can get them done in time," Lucy replied, surprised at how easy it was to talk with Mason. *It's his whole, Daddy, thing he has going on;* she said to herself as he led her to a park bench on top of a hill. The sky was turning a light shade of purple as the sun began to dip down, and Lucy shivered as the park lights came on.

"Are you cold, here," Mason said, taking off his jacket and placing it over Lucy's shoulders.

"Why are you so perfect?" Lucy asked, making Mason laugh.

"Oh, I'm far from perfect. But I can't have my, baby girl, going cold, can I?" He replied. They watched the runners in the park finish their daily exercise before speaking again. Mason had enjoyed the comfortable silence between them. He liked that Lucy didn't feel the need to fill the silence with pointless talking, that she was just happy being in the presence of each other.

"I could just stay here all night," Lucy said, leaning over and resting her head on Mason's shoulder. He moved his arm and held her, bring her closer to his side and kissing her forehead.

"But what about pizza?" He asked in a somber tone, reminding Lucy how they planned to check out a new pizza place which had been given fantastic reviews.

"Ok, I would leave for pizza, but not much

else," Lucy said, making Mason laugh as he stood.

"We'd better go, I'm not a fan of parks late at night," he said, holding out his hand to Lucy who accepted quickly.

"What, are you scared?" Lucy playfully asked.

"Yes, actually. And if you knew what happened here after dark, you'd be afraid as well," Mason said in a tone which made Lucy wonder what did go on out here after dark.

The walked the five blocks to the restaurant, Mason being greeted by an Italian man who sat them at the best table which overlooked the city.

"Woah, it is beautiful up here," Lucy said, looking over the city's lights.

"We keep this table reserved for only the best of our customers," the man said, taking the napkin and placing it over her lap. Lucy waited until he had walked away before looking at Mason with a curiosity in her eye that made him concerned.

"How do they know we are good

customers?" Lucy asked, her eyes narrowing in on Mason.

"It must just be the beautiful girl I am with. You know what the Italians are like, they know how to appreciate beauty," he replied, sipping his wine and watching fireworks light up the night's sky.

"I don't know how long I will stay teaching at school, Lucy," Mason suddenly said, causing Lucy to whip her head around to look at him.

"What do you mean?" She said, in a pouty voice she used before she could catch it to stop it.

"Well. I think I need to cut back my hours. I thought that I could manage, but it's just a lot right now," Mason said, taking a slice of his pizza and enjoying the cool night's breeze on his face. Lucy ate in silence, thinking of how to gain the information she wanted.

"You mean, between teaching and your other business?" She asked, taking a sip of her wine. Mason just nodded his head. He wasn't going to tell her that he was the man behind the gangs and mob who ran the city. Mason placed his hand on Lucy's thigh and parted her legs slightly.

"You ask a lot of questions my darling, that can be a dangerous thing," he said, the warning in his tone unmistakable. Lucy just nodded and looked down into her lap and bit her tongue. The last thing she wanted was to annoy this obviously powerful man in front of her.

"If you're finished, let's get out of here. I have something special planned," Mason said, taking Lucy's hand and leaving the restaurant. Mason took Lucy's hand and playfully ran up the street with her, jumping on a cable car as it moved up a hill.

"You're exciting," Lucy said puffing and laughing at the same time.

"Well, if you think this is exciting wait till you see the top," Mason said, winking at Lucy and holding her close as the cable car moved into the hills. Passing the homes with the multiple levels and cars Lucy had only seen in magazines, they climbed the steep incline, stopping once they had reached the top.

"Have you ever seen anything as wonderful as the view from up here? It overlooks the whole city, you can see everyone who keeps the pulse of the beast moving and everyone who tries to destroy it," Mason said, coming to stand behind Lucy and wrap his arms over her shoulders. She had to admit; he sure knew how to seduce a girl. They stood there, watching as the city moved below them. The iconic buildings which had always made Lucy feel insignificant now appearing as a mere contribution to the array of lights which dotted the city.

"You know, a house right here would be lovely," Lucy said, making Mason laugh.

"Yeah, and right behind us I would place a huge fire pit so that when we would sit out here and watch the world turn, we would have warmth on our backs," he replied, causing Lucy to look at him with her mischievous eyes.

"Hey, I have an idea," she said, pulling away from him and running towards the forest. Mason followed, worried about what she would find in those dark woods.

"Lucy, be careful," he said with fear in his voice. Lucy hadn't realized he could be scared, and it turned her on to know that she meant so much to him that he would worry.

"Where are you going?" He said, reaching out to grab her hand. She turned into him and kissed his lips suddenly.

"This would be where our bedroom would be," Lucy said, taking off her jacket and placing it on the floor.

"And here, our bed," she said, making Mason laugh and take off his jacket, placing it down next to Lucy's.

"Um, sweetheart, you are on my side of the bed," Mason said, rolling on top of her and making her giggle.

"Oh, here, let me make it up to you," she replied, kissing him again and moaning into his mouth.

"Really? Right here?" Mason said as Lucy

pulled her dress up to show him she wasn't wearing panties. She just bit her bottom lip and nodded as Mason excitedly unbuckled his belt and opened his pants.

"Do you want me to help, Daddy?" Lucy said, reaching out to touch his hardening cock. Mason just grabbed both her hands and held them above her head as he jerked himself off, getting hard as he watched Lucy's tits sway with each wriggle she made trying to escape his hand which secured hers.

"Don't make a sound," Mason instructed as he used his other hand to spread her pussy lips and tease her clit.

"Daddy is going to get you wet, little one," Mason said as he watched Lucy try to stay silent as he flicked her sensitive clit over and over until she was bucking her hips, craving for him to be inside of her.

"Now you're ready for Daddy," he said, pushing his cock into her tight cunt and laying his body on top of hers as he forced her to take him.

"You are such a good girl," Mason said, staying on top of her but pulling out slightly just to ram her again, feeling her big soft tits on his chest and her breathing coming out in short sharp gasps each time he filled her. Placing a hand over her mouth, Mason let her hands go and watched how Lucy played with her tits as he fucked her with more aggression than he knew she was ready for.

"Just a little longer, you can do that can't you baby," Mason said more than asked as he fucked her hard, holding both her hips down as he watched her tummy push out by the cock he forced into her over and over. Cumming, Mason sighed in relief, worried that Lucy would end their fun before he had been able to. Staying inside of her as he creamed her hole, Mason smirked as Lucy gasped, shocked that he would fill her with so much cum.

"Daddy, I'm not wearing any panties!" Lucy hissed, worried about the cum that would leak from her cunt. Mason just laughed as he pulled out a pull up from the deep pocket of his jacket.

"Then it's a good thing Daddy is prepared, isn't it," he said, pulling it up her thighs and around her waist.

"No one will even notice, your dress isn't tight around your ass, so you're good to go," Mason said reassuringly. Lucy just gave a sigh and rolled into Mason's arms as they watched the night's sky, Mason doing his pants back up in case someone accidentally came across them.

"Did you think that we would have such a good time? Like, have you had this much fun with other girls?" Lucy asked, kissing Mason's cheek.

"Honestly, no. I'm surprised; you are everything that I was looking for. I actually wanted to talk to you about that. You might hear some shit about me with other girls or whatever, but that's just coz girls can get a bit, crazy, when I break it off with them. So, just know that you are my only baby girl right now and that if you do hear some shit, it's just some old ex trying to stir up shit, ok?" Mason said, smiling at Lucy. She just looked up at him and nodded her head, happy that her Daddy was all hers.

Chapter 10

Lucy walked along the hallway to her lecture room in a hurry. She was late. It had been raining, and the roads were slippery as she rode her bike into college. As she approached the room, Ella stepped out from behind the wall.

"So, you're his new pet, hey?" She bitterly said. Lucy just rolled her eyes and tried to walk around her.

"I don't think so," Ella said, grabbing Lucy's hair and pulling her backward.

"I'm talking to you," Ella said, putting her hands on her hips.

"And I'm late," Lucy said, trying to get past again.

"You know. He said you were different," Ella said, causing Lucy to stop and turn to face her.

"Who are you talking about?" She said, hoping that this Ella wasn't the one with all the deeds to her name.

"Mason," Ella said, a hint of victory in her voice.

"You're, *Ella*," Lucy almost whispered, putting two and two together. Ella just stood there, wondering what Lucy was thinking.

"Yeah. We used to be mates until you came in and sweep Mason off his feet. Didn't he tell you about me? I had thought it was weird he had brought you into the café I work at. I thought it was to rub it in my face. But you don't know, do you? You have no idea who you are fucking?" Ella said, softening as she saw Lucy didn't understand her role in the whole situation.

"That's what he did with me when we first got together as well. Bought me all the things I had only ever dreamt of, took me to places I had only seen in movies. We even went to Paris in the fall and Milan in the spring. He does that, seduces you with a dream," Ella said, somewhat hoping that she was crushing Lucy.

"So, what changed?" Lucy asked, looking

down on the ground.

"What changed? You are what has changed. Before you life was great. Now I've been cut off, and the only person who takes my calls is Ellen, and I fucking hate that bitch," Ella scoffed. Lucy looked up and frowned.

"What's wrong with Ellen?" Lucy asked.

"She's weird as fuck. She wanted to dress me up as a baby and stuff. Fucking weird," Ella said, crossing her arms over her chest. Lucy just snorted, trying to suppress her laugh.

"Yeah, that's really weird," she replied, gaining an approving nod from Ella.

"So, what. You want me to end things with Mason?" Lucy questioned, taking out her phone and dialing his number.

"Yeah, I guess," Ella said, putting her hands on her hips again. Lucy pressed call, hearing Mason's phone go off inside the lecture theatre and the students laugh.

"Daddy, Ella's told me everything, and she is blocking my way into class. I'll be at home if you want to talk," Lucy said, hanging up the phone and putting it back in her pocket before Mason could reply. Shocked, Ella lunged at Lucy but copping a sucker punch to her stomach as Lucy blocked her.

"Don't fuck with me again," Lucy whispered in Ella's ear as she lay doubled over on the floor before turning around and heading home.

Lucy didn't have to wait long before Mason was calling her phone, but ignoring him, Lucy went for a jog. When she got back, she was surprised to see Mason standing in the living room, Ellen and Alfred on the couch and who she had supposed was Cherry standing by the fireplace.

"Lucy, come and sit down," Ellen said affectionately.

"No, you're all scaring me," Lucy said, trying to back away just to have Mason grab her wrist and fling her onto the couch and into Ellen's waiting arms.

"Now now, there's no need for that," Ellen said, rocking Lucy loving as she tried to calm her.

"What did Ella tell you?" Mason barked. Lucy hadn't heard him use that voice before, and it scared her. Storming over to her, Mason grabbed her chin in his hands and shook her head.

"What did she say!?" He yelled, getting slapped away by Ellen, who held Lucy as she cried into her ample breasts.

"It's imperative that we know sweetie," Ellen said stroking Lucy's hair down.

"She just said that you are with her too!" Lucy spat back at Mason before burying her face in Ellen's breasts once more. Mason sighed, put his hands on his head before reaching out for Lucy, who just flinched and pulled away from him.

"I don't want a Daddy like you," Lucy said, sucking her thumb and looking out at him with broken-hearted eyes. Mason looked around the room at the others, gauging their approval of what he wanted to tell her next. As he made eye contact with each of the other members of his family, each nodding their head to him, he came over to sit next to Lucy who again, pulled away from him.

"Lucy. I need to explain everything to you," he said, gently resting his hand on her leg.

"But before I do, I have to tell you that, I will have to kill you if you say this to anyone," Mason said making Lucy roll her eyes.

"That what? You run game internationally for the two biggest families in the state? I already know that I've known that for weeks," Lucy said, impressed with herself. Speechless, Mason grew cautious.

"Daddy, I tapped your laptop, phone and um, jacket and car," Lucy said, making he equally as amused as mad.

"Here, let me show you," Lucy said, folding the collar of his jacket down and pulling off a stick on transmitter.

"Are you telling me...that we got hoodwinked by an undergrad college girl?" Ellen said, looking directly at Mason.

"I'm very smart, Aunty Ellen," Lucy said matter of factly.

"Too smart," Mason said, shaking his head.

"I like this front you've got; it works really well. But it's too easy to get in. Your cock got you in this mess. Good thing I'm such a good girl," Lucy said, kissing a still shocked Mason on the cheek.

"It always does," Alfred said, going into the kitchen and pouring himself a scotch.

"So, what now?" Lucy said making everyone turn to look at her.

"What do you mean, what now?" Mason said before shaking his head at her.

"No. Don't even think about it. You aren't getting involved. I'm keeping you exactly how you are. My beautiful college student baby girl," Mason said, causing Lucy to roll her eyes.

"But Daddy," Lucy said, making Cherry laugh. Mason just picked Lucy up in his arms and held her tight, not wanting ever to let her go.

"I'm sorry if I hurt you baby girl. I kind of thought maybe you were with the FBI or CIA or something," Mason said taking her into the bedroom.

"Would an agent of the law do this," Lucy

said, pulling on his belt buckle and ripping down his pants as she lay tummy down on the bed.

"No, I don't think so," Mason said, cupping her jaw in his hand and sliding his cock into her mouth, only stopping when her eyes started to water. As Lucy's swallowed around his cock, Mason gasped as he felt Lucy's throat open for the first time and take him deeper, almost making his knees weak. Just as Mason began fucking her face harder, Lucy pulled her head back and giggled.

"Nope, not feeling it, Daddy," she said, making Mason look at her in shock. He watched as Lucy got off the bed, laughing as she ran into the office. Following, Mason stopped when he saw her laying on the desk, her hair hanging down the side of the desk.

"I changed my mind again, I'm ready for you now," Lucy said, making Mason laugh and jump up on the desk, pressing his body down on hers.

"God, you feel so good," he said as he pulled Lucy's panties to the side, spitting on his cock and pushed it inside of her.

"Yeah, this is what I want," Mason said, fucking her excitedly. He pounded her as her moans filled the room, echoed down the hall, and reached the living room.

"Well, I guess he's welcoming her to the family," Ellen said with a smirk on her face. Alfred and Cherry, both just nodded in acceptance of Mason's decision and got up to leave, turning back to see Ellen. She just sighed as she pulled out her phone.

"No, I get to make the call now, we have to deal with Ella," Ellen said, slightly annoyed that the aftermath of that girl was still something she was sorting out.

"You know that this opens us up to getting attacked by the Irish. Having Paddy's daughter was our guarantee of hassle-free transport," Alfred said plainly.

"Yes. I am wildly aware Alfred," Ellen said snapping at him, shutting him down. Alfred and Cherry, knowing that their contribution to this meeting was over, left the apartment just as Mason strolled through the living room with a sheet around his waist.

"Oh, modesty is a wasted look on you," Ellen mocked, watching as Mason dropped his towel.

"Better?" He asked, swinging his cock from side to side and coping a narrowed eyed glare from Ellen.

"I'm sending Ella home with enough cash and coke to buy Paddy's forgiveness, hopefully," Ellen said knowing how important it was for Mason to maintain the open ports to move the guns through Irish territory to the Italians.

"Ellen, I would be lost without you," Mason said, coming to kiss her on the cheek but getting his dick slapped instead.

"Don't pretend you don't like it," Ellen said, standing up and walking to find Lucy to get her cleaned up and turned back into the baby Ellen loved so much.

Chapter 11

"Baby girl, where are you?" Ellen called through the apartment, looking for Lucy. Hearing her giggles, Ellen walked into the bedroom and saw Lucy rolling on the bed naked.

"Come on, sweetie, let's get you in the bath for Daddy," Ellen said as Mason ran into the bedroom pretending to be a plane.

"Daddy!" Lucy said making Ellen roll her eyes and walk out of the room.

"So, let's put in, all the toys tonight," Mason said, tipping all the bath toys into the big tub splashing the water over the side of the bath making Lucy laugh.

"Daddy, you are so silly," Lucy giggled splashing around the tub.

"Oh this is nice and warm," Mason said shivering in the tub as his body adjusted to the temperature.

"Daddy, let's play hairdressers," Lucy said, swimming over to him and climbing on his lap, putting his hair in a Mohawk and finishing the look with bubbles on top. Mason laughed, reaching for his phone and snapping silly photos of his new hairstyle.

"Oh yeah baby girl, Daddy looks good!" He laughed, before sinking to the bottom of the tub and coming back up aggressively, splashing more water onto the bathroom floor.

"Lucy?" Mason asked, seeing her playing quietly with a bucket and spade. He watched as she scooped water into the bucket and then pretended to make a cake, mixing the water and bubbles and together.

"How'd I get so lucky," Mason said, sitting back against the far side of the tub and relaxing. He watched for another 20 minutes, getting out when the water turned cold.

"Come on, if we stay in there much longer we'll get sick," Mason said, holding Lucy's hooded bunny towel and smiling as she let him put it on her.

"Cute," he said, taking her back into her bedroom and laying her on the bed. Obediently, Lucy lifted her bottom up and let Mason diaper her, tickling her as he stuck the tabs down. He dressed her in her white teddy bear onesie and carried her back out into the living room, looking around for Ellen, who had left a message on a note on the table.

I've gone to clean up a mess, the note read, Mason smiling as he knew precisely what Ellen was referring to, or rather, who Ellen was referring to.

"Well, I guess it's just you and me for the night baby girl," Mason said, opening the fridge to see what they could eat for dinner.

"What about this risotto?" He asked, looking back to see Lucy nodding her head as she colored. She lay on her tummy, her legs swinging in the air as she decorated a page by the fireplace. Mason smiled; he hadn't felt so relaxed in years. He wasn't sure what it was, but something about taking care of a girl like this made him feel so important and needed. It wasn't about the power or control for Mason; it was about someone seeing him as excellent and kind when he knew that the things he had done in his life were anything but kind.

"Here you go," Mason said, taking Lucy's pink glitter bowl and filling it with the warmed risotto. He sat next to her and let her climb into his lap before he began feeding her, loving how she rested her head on his shoulder, snuggling as she ate.

"Daddy has to go out on business soon little one. I'll be gone for a week. No, I won't be with Ella. I've already had her taken off the deeds so; you have nothing to worry about. I'll get Ellen to look after you, alright?" Mason explained, Lucy just nodding her head and reaching for her blankie. Mason held her, and he leaned forward and grabbed it, waiting for Lucy to snuggle back into him before continuing to feed her.

"Daddy, can we go shopping online tonight,

please? I've seen some really cute things I'd love and since you won't be here next week," Lucy said, looking up at Mason with the cheeky smile he loved so much.

"Oh, are you trying to make Daddy feel bad for leaving you?" Mason playfully teased.

"Well no, but if that's how you feel Daddy," Lucy giggled, wriggling out of his arms.

"Can we make a blankie fort and then lay in it when we look at things?" Lucy asked, getting surprised when Mason flung all the cushions up into the air and began designing the fort.

"No, Daddy. It has to go over here," Lucy said, drawing a picture of how she wanted the fort to look.

After an hour of pillow fights, giggling and playing ghosts with the blankies, Lucy and Mason finally had the fort designed and were laying on the pillow bed they had made, looking up at the stars Lucy had made and cut out, sticking them to the ceiling with tape.

"Ok, here, show Daddy what you would like,

baby girl," Mason said, passing Lucy his tablet. She flicked through various sites, adding things to her shopping carts as Mason watched her. She selected a variety of new onesies and socks, pacifiers and stuffies. She looked at Mason who just laughed and took the tablet from her hands and clicked buy now, surprised that Lucy hadn't spent over $2000.

"You are so adorable. I don't mind you spending Daddy's money baby girl," Mason said, before going onto another site and clicking through their stock as Lucy fell asleep on his chest.

When Lucy woke, it was late morning, and as she rolled around the blankie fort, Mason was nowhere to be found. Feeling the pit of her stomach drop, she slowly made her way out of the fort and rubbed her eyes sleepily.

"There she is," Mason said, making Lucy instantly happy and relieved that he hadn't gone yet.

"I thought you'd left Daddy," Lucy said, coming over to cuddle him.

"No, not yet. But I will have to go after breakfast. Sit down at the table; your waffles are almost ready," Mason instructed. Lucy walked over to the table and sat down by her coloring in book and crayons.

"Daddy, I love you," Lucy said, making Mason drop the waffle he was moving from the hot plate to his plate. Giggling, Lucy just sipped her juice from her sippy cup and watched as Mason tried to get his head around what she had just said.

"You love me?" He asked, almost not believing her. Lucy just nodded her head and smiled.

"Yep. I love you, Daddy," Lucy repeated, making Mason beam with joy and run over to her to kiss her on both her cheeks.

"You have made me so happy," Mason said, returning to the kitchen and putting a new waffle on his plate and walking to the table.

"You should probably feed yourself this morning sweetie, have to get you back into your big girl space, or you'll have a tough time going into town," Mason said, pouring syrup over Lucy's waffle.

"Why do I have to go into town, Daddy?" Lucy asked Mason, who was already halfway through his breakfast.

"I have a few things that I bought you, and I want you to go and get them yourself. I was thinking that it would make you feel special to walk around town carrying all your bags," Mason said, putting his fork down and kissing the top of Lucy's forehead before getting up to put more waffles on his plate. Lucy just looked at Mason, his muscular shoulders, loving eyes, and boyish grin. The way his hair swayed when it was not styled and smiled as she thought about how different he looked when he was the in control Mason in public compared to how he was when he was her Daddy in private.

"Done?" Mason asked, pulling Lucy from her daydream and taking her plate away.

"Yeah, thanks," Lucy said, unzipping her onesie and stripping right there in the middle of the dining room.

"Well, that didn't take long," Mason laughed, coming back and picking up the clothes and diaper Lucy had left on the floor.

"I'm just going to have a shower, be right back," Lucy said, slapping Mason on the ass playfully as she passed him making him look at her with a smirk on his face.

"How did it go with the Irish?" Mason asked Ellen as Alfred drove him to the airport.

"As good as expected. They want their product, though. They don't understand why they have to wait," Ellen said.

"They have to wait because I fucking told them too. And because we haven't got it yet. Did you tell them I'm personally going to go get it and that they'll have it within the week?" Mason asked, drinking scotch and offering one to Ellen who accepted.

"Yes, of course, I did," Ellen replied, sipping her drink.

"Good. See, everyone will get Christmas on the same day," Mason said as they arrived at his private jet.

"Give this to Lucy," Mason said, passing Ellen a box which had a pair of earrings.

"Make sure she does her homework and goes to class," Mason said before laughing and getting out of the car.

"This is going to work, isn't it?" Alfred said to Ellen as they watched Mason get onto the plane before driving away.

"It has too; we have all spent too many years working on getting to this point," Ellen said, opening the box and looking at the earrings.

"And Lucy?" Alfred said, watching Ellen from the rear vision mirror.

"She's innocent of all of this, and that is how we are going to keep it," Ellen said assertively, looking directly at Alfred who just nodded and turned back to watch the road.

"Anyway. We made all the mistakes on Ella; Lucy will not be any trouble," Ellen said, more to herself than to Alfred.

Chapter 12

"Ellen, I think someone is following me," Lucy softly said as she hid in a restaurants bathroom.

"Where are you?" Ellen said, getting up from the couch and snapping her fingers at Alfred.

"At, *Hello Chicki*, I'm in the bathroom," Lucy nervously said. Ellen had been fearful of this. That the Irish would take Lucy as an insurance that they would get their product.

"This is what I need you to do. Go to sit at a table closest to the cash register and wait there for me," Ellen said, running with Alfred to the car and getting in, closing the door as the car sped out of the garage and onto the street.

"I'm scared," Lucy said, making Ellen want to be there already.

"Tell me what the men looked like," Ellen said, wanting to give Lucy a job, so she didn't feel so useless.

"Well, they were in dark jeans, and both had raggedy looking jackets, and they kept going into all the stores I was going into. One asked me if I was having a good day, but I just smiled at him and nodded my head," Lucy replied.

"Good, so you didn't speak with them?" Ellen clarified as they turned into the street Lucy was on.

"No. I thought maybe they were waiting to see if it was me by my tongue piercing," Lucy said, making Ellen smile.

"Clever girl. Yeah, if they haven't taken you by now, they either are unsure it's you and want that clarification, or they are just trying to warn us that they can get close to us. Either way, I'm here now," Ellen said walking into the restaurant and sitting down at the table where Lucy was and turning to see the two men who were following Lucy walk in and search for her. Getting up, Ellen held Lucy's hand as she walked to the men.

"Tell Paddy, it's on the way and that

stalking an innocent civilian won't make the shipment happen any faster," Ellen said in a voice Lucy hadn't heard before. It was hard and angry, and the type of voice Lucy was happy had never been used on her.

"Get in," Ellen said, opening the door for Lucy who quickly scurried into the back seat, happy to be safe.

"Maybe don't go shopping on your own anymore," Ellen suggested, peering into the bags and raising an eyebrow.

"Mason bought me them," Lucy said, feeling her face go red which just amused Ellen.

"Who were those guys?" Lucy asked, looking at Ellen but was surprised when Alfred started speaking.

"They are from the Irish mob. Dangerous, dangerous men. You were right to ring us; they would have waited until you weren't in such a public place and then have taken you, holding you captive until Mason delivers," he said.

"It was good that you weren't going to some

club or quiet art gallery. I hate to admit it, but once they have you, they disappear like ghosts. We wouldn't have got you back before we delivered and even then, you'd have been changed," Alfred said, a sadness in his voice.

"How do you know so much about the way they work?" Lucy asked, making Alfred slam on his brakes. He turned around to face Lucy and pulled up his sleeve, revealing a grotesque scar that encircled most of his forearm.

"I used to hunt them down, this is a souvenir from those times," he said before turning back around and continuing to drive, leaving Lucy speechless as she looked out the window for the rest of the ride home. *What did he mean, he used to chase them? What is this life I am getting involved in? Is it worth it? I mean, I only wanted some extra money to get me through college,* Lucy thought as they pulled into the garage of Mason's home.

"I think it's best if you stay with us until Mason gets back," Ellen said, Lucy just nodding her head.

"I know you've got classes you need to go to, do you have a burning desire to go onto campus or would you be interested in doing the degree online?" She continued making Lucy's head spin.

"Um, I guess I could do it online. I mean, the goal was to make a lot of money with the qualifications I got there. But I kinda think that I'm good. In fact, I don't really like the degree anyway," Lucy said, surprising herself as the truth she hadn't truly admitted to herself now came to the surface.

"So, what are you going to do?" Ellen asked. Lucy just shook her head.

"I don't know. Let me think about it," she replied, taking her things and walking to Mason's room.

She placed her bags down by his bed and climbed into his side, snuggling into his pillow and smelling his cologne on the sheets. *What are my options?* Lucy thought to herself, closing her eyes and trying to picture her life. She imaged, doing her uni degree online. *But for what?* She thought as she opened her eyes again. She was only going to college because she thought that she needed to to get a high paying job to finance her life. *Could I be a part of the family?* She said to herself, looking down at the gifts she had been given from Mason, his only request that she be his baby when he wanted and his girlfriend when he needed somewhere to stick his cock. *It's not a bad life,* Lucy said to herself, biting her bottom lip and making her decision. *I mean, I could do Intel, I'm good at that,* Lucy thought walking out into the garden. She walked through the grounds, enjoying the sculpted bushes and colorful flowers and stopping when she found a table and chair set up by the far end of the property.

"Life was simpler then. Boring, broke, but simpler," Lucy said as she saw Alfred coming to look for her.

"Are you having doubts? If you are, it is better you get out now. Mason will understand. He won't cause you any trouble," he said, sitting down next to Lucy. He had brought a thermos of coffee and poured two cups, handing one to her.

"It's just that, I don't want to be a kept house pet," Lucy said, watching as the man nodded his head.

"The thing is, you wouldn't have to worry about this if you haven't snooped around looking for answers. Your conflict doesn't come from deciding to go to college or not; it comes from deciding if you want to blood in or not. It comes from not being sure what position you will have and how your days will go once you step into this life," Alfred knowingly said. Lucy just looked at him while he spoke.

"That's exactly right. It's also not knowing the rules when I can ask questions, what it all means," Lucy said, wishing she didn't sound so pathetic.

"That will all come with time. I have a feeling; Mason will want you to keep studying. You will study law. These are his wishes if you want to stay. He hopes that you will. You'll study law, own a couple of businesses that will make your life easily justifiable. You can have everything you ever wanted Lucy, all you have to do is, take the call," Alfred said, patting her on the shoulder as he passed her and walked back towards the house. Lucy stayed sitting and drinking the coffee, wondering if she was lucky or not. The family wasn't like what she thought they would be; they weren't like the gangster's in the movies. She took out her phone and ended her relationship with the two other sugar Daddies she had, happy that they were too far away to have ever touched her and looked up at the sky.

"It's about to get real," Lucy said out loud as she looked at the clouds moving overhead. She picked up the thermos and cups, got up from her chair and began to walk back up to the house, just as the sun dipped behind the hills.

Lucy stayed at Mason's house for the rest of the week, dropping out of her degree and enrolling through an online university in Law. Mason had been over the moon when she had told him the night he got back.

"Wow, you would really do that? That's amazing!" He said, jumping up from the table and kissing Lucy full on the mouth. He smelt like the jungle and tasted like dirt, Lucy pulling away and looking at him with a puzzled expression.

"I know, I should have had a shower first, but I was just so hungry for a real meal," Mason said, reaching out to hold her hand.

"How come, you've been so successful?" Lucy asked as Mason finished his burger. He looked at her with a curious expression.

"What do you mean?" He questioned, unsure of her meaning.

"Well, how come you never get caught by the feds? Aren't they always after you?" Lucy asked, eating the last of her nuggets.

"Do you know how, when you go to watch a play, you only see the actors?" Mason started explaining, looking at Lucy and smiling at her sweetly.

"Yeah," Lucy slowly replied, enjoying the

metaphor.

"Well, the actors are told where to go, what to dress in, how to speak and even portrayed not by their own hand, but by the people backstage. When a play goes bad, it's the cast who gets blamed; no one even thinks about the people backstage, just the two main characters and the whole play is a hit or miss depending on those two people. It's the same thing here," Mason said, getting up to get the soda he left on the kitchen bench.

"Plus, I'm not tied to anything, and everyone is frazzled once a pattern is broken. Our family breaks the pattern. Instead of having a bunch of tough young thugs, we have three mature aged people and me. And for anyone looking in, it looks like I am a successful real estate investor, and they are the people who look after me. You're my girlfriend, and while all of that is true, who we are backstage is completely different," Mason continued to explain.

"Why doesn't everyone do it like this," Lucy

asked, taking a sip of Mason's drink.

"Because of ego. They want to be the King, the big dog. I just want to get rich, so I can disappear when and how I want," Mason said, watching as Lucy nodded her head.

"So, this is what we are going to do. I'm going to sell you the apartment you are living in; you are going to be my girlfriend by day, my baby girl by night. You study law online because you are too busy working at, where would you like to work?" Mason said, stopping and looking at Lucy who just shrugged her shoulders.

"You like fashion, tech, and jewelry? You want to own a bar? A club?" Mason said, giving Lucy suggestions.

"Maybe in fashion, that's cool," Lucy said, excited about what the future was going to have in store for her.

"Ok, so we make you your own clothing label. Then you work there, and we live happily ever after," Mason said, finishing off Lucy's fries.

"I had no idea life could be like this, I had no

idea everything could be so easy," she exclaimed, shocked that she had been handed her life on a silver platter, and even more shocked that it was so easy.

"Life doesn't have to be hard, that's a choice everyone makes," Mason said, stretching his arms out wide.

"And I don't want to make that choice," he added, opening his palm to Ellen who placed a gun in his hand.

"Excuse me, darling, I need to take out the trash," Mason said, standing up and walking towards the back of the house. Lucy watched as he left, smiled to herself, and began designing what kind of clothes she wanted to sell, surprised that Mason's business didn't scare or unsettled her at all.

Chapter 13

Lucy had been working on her outfit designs for a weeks before Mason sent them overseas to be developed.

"Do you think they will understand the direction I want to take with them," she asked over their breakfast. Mason had taken her to a new café which had opened in their neighboring suburb, and over champagne and strawberries, bagels and waffles, Mason had shown her the emails between him and their production warehouse.

"This is so cool; I can't believe that a mere 8months ago, I was some lost college student with nothing but debt and then you came in and saved me like a princess," Lucy said, appealing to his need to save people. Mason had recently begun growing a beard, and Lucy liked that he was even more sensual and dashing.

"Well, I couldn't have all your potential

going to waste could I?" He replied, reaching into his jacket to take out a necklace box.

"Open it," Mason said, sitting back in his chair and gesturing to the waiter to refill his glass. Lucy looked at Mason with playful suspicion and opened the box to see a thread of brilliant-cut diamonds set in rose gold.

"Oh my god," Lucy gushed, surprised that he would buy her such an extravagant gift.

"I was hoping you would wear it to the opening of your shop next month," Mason said, smiling at Lucy and standing up to clasp the diamond collar around her neck.

"It's so beautiful, it would be an honor," Lucy replied, touching her new neckpiece.

"Normally, when there's a community or something, a collaring would take place publically, but, it's just you and me kid. So I was wondering, if you wanted, would you consider wearing it after your opening, as a symbol that you belong to me and that no one can take better care of you than I can?" Mason asked. Lucy hadn't seen him so nervous before. She had read up on collaring ceremonies and smiled lovingly at Mason, her eyes already telling him the answer he wanted.

"I want nothing more than to be yours, Daddy," Lucy said, leaning forward and whispering in his ear, placing her freshly manicured hand on his thigh and kissing his cheek before pulling away from him. Mason had taught Lucy how he liked to be adored and worshipped, how he wanted to be greeted in the morning and how he liked his woman to behave and just like the loyal and obedient girl that Lucy was, she had passed every one of his tests with flying colors.

"Good. In that case, we will have to get you a dress to match this beautiful collar," Mason said, standing and holding his hand out to Lucy.

"Shall we, my dear?" He asked, admiring the way Lucy walked in her 6-inch heels.

"I do believe we shall," Lucy replied, tipping their waitress before walking out, her hand held by Mason who walked in front of her.

They walked down the street, going into one shop

after another and coming out disappointed continuously with the range of dresses that were on offer.

"Honestly, how hard is it to make a nice dress?" Mason snarled as they exited the fifth store.

"Daddy, I have an idea," Lucy said, taking his hand and leading him down a back street.

"How do you know about this place?" Mason asked, surprised that they were now deep in Italian territory.

"Hello, darling!" A man exclaimed upon Lucy walking into his store; the man all but bowed to Mason who tried not to laugh at the flamboyant gesture and proceeded to walk through the store.

"I need a dress. It's for my store's opening," Lucy said as Mason sat down on a comfortable chair.

"Certainly," the man said, spinning around the room and collecting a handful of dresses before pushing Lucy into a changing room and waiting outside.

"It means a lot for you to come into my store. I am aware of who you are. I am surprised, this could be seen as taking sides," the man said speaking to Mason.

"It is not taking sides. We will get the entertainment from the Irish; you will dress me. You will both be invited. This will be a civil event, seeing as my store is in both of your territories," Lucy said, making the man's eyes widen.

"I see," he said, turning to face Mason who acted as though it was his idea.

"I am to assume you have spoken to all involved parties?" The man asked, turning back to Lucy.

"I have. Ella, Sophia, Danielle, and Skye are all coming, and I've extended the invite to their fathers," Lucy said, knowing the weight behind the words she spoke. This was a political move. She had become acquaintances with the daughters of the four most powerful families who ran not only the Italian and Irish mobs but the commissioner's daughter as well as the daughter of the candidate who was running for office. She knew that bringing these families together, under one roof, would put her in the limelight and Mason smiled as he watched her become the lady boss he had thought she could be.

"Well, it would be an honor," the man repeated as Lucy came out in a dress that blew Mason away. Involuntarily standing, Mason saw Lucy as a woman for the first time and cleared his throat.

"I thought so too," Lucy said, smirking and turning away from him to look back in the mirror.

"We will take this one," she said to the man who nodded enthusiastically.

"That is an excellent choice," he said, as Lucy went back into the changing rooms to take the masterpiece of a dress off.

"I didn't know you know those girls," Mason said as they walked back down the alley and out onto the main street.

"I don't really, but watch this," Lucy said,

dialing a number on her phone.

"Ella. It's Lucy, don't hang up. There is going to be a new store opening, and I think it could be beneficial to your family. Danielle has already confirmed she will be there; I thought if she were going to be there, it would be more than fitting for you also to attend," Lucy said. *As smooth as butter,* Mason thought, smirking as Ella went quiet on the phone.

"You know family is everything to me, I'll be there, send me the details," Ella said before hanging up the phone.

"Now, to call Skye," Lucy said, sitting on a sidewalk bench and dialing Skye's number.

"How do you have all their contacts?" Mason asked. Lucy just laughed and rolled her eyes.

"I hacked their phones," she said in a matter of fact tone that made Mason wrap his arm around her.

"Skye, Lucy, how are you? Look, I'm not going to beat around the bush. Some stuff is going down, and your Father will want in. I'm sending you the details to an event, make sure you are both there, I mean if you want to win that is," Lucy said, rolling her eyes as Skye began to stutter.

"Who are you?" Skye asked in an innocent voice Mason remembered Lucy having.

"A friend. A friend who can get you everything you want, including Danielle. You being gay is this town's worst kept secret honey," Lucy said, hearing a soft giggle from the other end of the phone.

"Ok, we'll be there," Skye said, Lucy, sticking her tongue out victoriously.

"She's a lesbian?" Mason asked.

"Yeah, I saw her profile last year. Cute really. Too bad her dad's so homophobic. We can work on that too," Lucy said, ringing Danielle.

"Hey, babe, you want some goss?" Lucy asked.

"Yeah," Danielle replied. Mason just sat back and placed both his hands on the back of his head.

"That cute girl from your summer camp last year is going to be at a store opening next month, here are the details. Oh, I've got my doctor calling me, bye," Lucy said, hanging up quickly.

"She isn't one to chat. I met her a few months ago when I went shopping. We bonded over our hatred of wedges," Lucy said, taking a breath for the first time in minutes.

"Ok, this is the tricky one," she said, finding Sophia's number.

"Sophia, hi," Lucy said. Sophia was the daughter of the commissioner and someone who played it safer than safe. Her one weakness, she needed to be needed.

"Look, I need a favor. I am having a store opening party, and I am anxious that no one will come, can I put you down as a guest, and you can bring as many people as you want as long as you are there. Please, Sophia?" Lucy said, her little voice escaping and making Mason laugh.

"Oh my god, yes you can count on me. I'll defs be there babe," Sophia said, making Lucy raise her eyebrow and look at Mason who just slowly clapped for her.

"Thank you so much. I have to go sorry babe; my doctor is calling me," Lucy said, hanging up the phone and smiling victoriously.

"So, now they are all coming," Lucy said, picking up her bag and standing up.

"Do you think you used the doctor line too much?" Mason asked, making Lucy scoff.

"No, I could have multiple doctors," she replied as they walked to the car Alfred had parked up the street.

"This is the new era, Daddy. Long gone are the days where real mobsters hang out in bars and whack people in alleys. The day is rising on us, and I fully intend on running it. The old guys can play their games, they can run their product and have their illegal operations, but it's through the media, politics and having a finger in every single fucking pie that will make us untouchable," Lucy said, making Mason more proud than he had ever been in her.

"You know. I made the right choice collaring you," he said, waving Alfred away and opening the door for Lucy.

"So, what is your next play?" Mason asked, catching Alfred's attention.

"We need to have a family meeting when we get home," Lucy said winking at Alfred.

"I get the feeling we are about to have a very exciting time," he said, making Lucy and Mason laugh.

"That's one way of putting it," Lucy said, turning to stare out the window as she thought through how to execute the next part of her plan.

Chapter 14

When they arrived at the house, Ellen and Cherry were already sitting on the couch with a pot of tea between them. They had obviously not been there very long by the way the pot was still steaming. These were the things Lucy noticed now. Before she would have just seen the two ladies sitting there, now she noticed that the curtains were drawn back but the room wasn't warm enough for them to have been open very long. The steam from the tea told Lucy that they had only just made it and their clothes, while linen, were not creased enough to have meant they had been there longer than 15 minutes.

"So, the baby has a play," Alfred said, walking into the room.

"Alfred, I'm only a baby at night. Please, credit where it is due," Lucy laughed sitting down and pouring herself a cup of tea.

"So, my store will be opening next month, which is only a week away. And you also know that it is smack bang in the middle of the Irish and Italian territories. We also know that things have been good between everyone for a while, but that they could be better. The Italians just had a raid on one of their warehouses, the Irish have had to go underground for various reasons. We also know that the commissioner wants to come down hard on the docks, and the candidate Williamson is making all sorts of promises about coming down hard on organized crime. These are troubling times," Lucy said, sipping her tea.

"If we wanted to hear a report we could turn on the news," Mason teased, wanting to know Lucy's plan. Lucy just looked at him the way he looked at her before she was about to get a spanking, which made him smirk even more.

"But what you have all taught me, is that no one suspects the break in the pattern," Lucy said, waiting for everyone to catch up with her.

"No one would suspect a bunch of girls

going to get their nails done at a store owned by an old woman," Lucy said, looking a Cherry who just narrowed her eyes at being called old but smirking as she saw the magnitude of potential Lucy's plan held.

"No one would suspect friends out on a shopping spree. If we hide in plain sight, giving the commissioner low-level criminals from rivaling or wannabee gangs, everyone wins," Lucy said, finishing her tea and looking around the room.

"I think this could work. Everyone is losing money right now, and our common enemy is us. It's our addiction to the struggle of power when we don't need to struggle at all," Lucy said.

"And your plan is to go through the daughters?" Ellen asked, clearly skeptical about the whole plan.

"Yep. Because everybody knows, a real Daddy never says no to his princess," Lucy said, smiling victoriously.

The evening of the store's opening had finally

arrived, and so had Ella, accompanied by her entourage. Danielle had come alone, just her security to back her up. Sophia was busy standing next to her father, and Skye was busy looking at Danielle. Greeting them one by one, Lucy led them into the back room of the store and watched as they took it all in.

"Gangster," Danielle remarked, nodding approvingly at Lucy.

"Ladies, have a seat," Lucy said. The four women sat around a round table in the luxurious entertainment room as a song played on the jukebox.

"So. I've invited you here tonight to first, welcome you into the store. But more pressingly, to talk business," Lucy said, looking around the table and into each women's eyes.

"We have all seen the headlines, and we all know whose fault it is that half our families are now incarcerated," Lucy said, looking directly at Skye.

"You know what, no, I am not about to sit

here and heard that it's my fault," Skye said, standing up.

"Sit your ass down," Lucy said in a way that made Skye's knees bend instantly.

"The problem is, they are using an old system to do business. Long gone are the days where trench coats and boats ran the city. We are in an era where it has never been easier to move large imports and exports. To catch bad guys in the act, or to win the hearts of the people," Lucy said.

"So this is what I suggest. You want your dad to win this election, right?" Lucy asked Skye, who nodded her head.

"Then you need something that is going to win the hearts of the people. Nothing wins elections like good marketing. So, we will keep his dirty secrets of going to illegal brothels on the border, and in return, you'll get your Daddy to hire one person from each our three families in prominent positions, I'll send you the list later," Lucy said, receiving a nod from Skye.

"I need you to leave the docks to your father and start a new trade route. We are going to be flying private from now on. You are going to sell all your real estate and start buying small, boring looking buildings under low-level associate's names, both of you," Lucy said, looking at Ella and Daniella.

"And you, oh you," Lucy said, looking at Sophia. Sophia knew her role in this would be significant. She also knew that Lucy had dirt on her if she was speaking, so openly in front of her.

"You'll take this. I'll send you details of crimes that your Daddy can organize to stop. He will be the hero this city deserves," Lucy said. Sophia just looked at Lucy before sighing and nodding her head.

"And what do you gain from all of this?" Ella asked. Lucy thought back nine months ago and almost laughed out loud that the dynamics of their relationship had shifted so dramatically.

"This isn't about me. This is about us. We run this city, not the families and not the cops. Us.

I'm so sick and tired of men telling me what my place is, that I need to have a good public presence that I can't step out of line because it will damage what their objectives are. They raised us to be ruthless, whether that's for good or for bad, that's up to you to decide. But while they were busy telling us how to live our lives, they forgot that made us invisible. And no one can catch a ghost," Lucy said, stirring in the other women a truth they had all long kept hidden.

"Look, guns, drugs, the rest of it, it's always been here, what is different now is that we have a say in how it gets organized," Lucy said, receiving agreement from the four women who sat at the table.

"Let's run this bitch," Sophia said, thinking about the heart attack her Father would have knowing she just got into bed with the enemy, knowing full well that is how he got to where he was.

"I want to be president," Skye said making the other women laugh.

"Then you'd better stick with us," Danielle replied, winking at her and making her blush.

"You know what this means?" Ella said to Lucy, who just nodded her head.

"We could become the biggest organization that this country has ever seen," Lucy replied, raising her glass to the women who sat in front of her.

"To a new era, to us," Lucy said, the other women joining with her in both excitement and quiet intensity. Walking back onto the store floor, they parted ways upon kissing each other's cheek.

"All good?" Mason said, coming over to Lucy who was looking through the clothes on the rack.

"Yes, it's going to be perfect," Lucy said before taking Mason's hand.

"But I'm tired, can we go home now, Daddy?" Lucy said, reaching for Mason's arm and cuddling into it. He just smiled before walking her out of the store, the cold night air hitting them like a slap on the face.

"I think it's so funny, you're my little gangster baby girl," Mason laughed as Lucy told him how the evening went.

"Everyone has their secrets. Daddy," Lucy said, reaching into her handbag and pulling out her pacifier.

"Look at you. Diamond collar, sexy dress, the highest heels I have ever seen, and a glittery pink paci. How are you so perfect, Lucy?" Mason said as she kicked off her heels and snuggled into him.

"I don't know, Daddy," Lucy replied from behind her pacifier.
The car pulled into the driveway, and Mason carried Lucy from the car like a princess. She never got tired of this, and dramatically posed in his arms, making him laugh.

"I don't want you to be my baby girl just yet, sweetheart," Mason gently whispered as he pulled Lucy's paci from her mouth.

"Do you want me to be your slutty girlfriend, Daddy?" Lucy sensually whispered in his ear.

"Yeah. You looked so good tonight; I want to do unspeakable things to you," Mason said, letting her drop out of his arms and onto his bed.

"How do you want me to start?" Lucy said, already knowing the answer. Mason unzipped his trousers and let his cock and balls hang in front of Lucy's mouth before pushing them against her lips, making himself hard as he used her.

"Just like that. Open wide for Daddy," Mason said, sticking his dick in Lucy's mouth, groaning as she sucked him deep, opening herself up to him as he pushed in further.

"God you've become so good, baby girl," Mason said, his eyes closing as he arched his back and lifted his arms above his head as he stretched.

"It was a risky move you made tonight, baby," Mason said as he fucked Lucy's face.

"Yeah, and it's about to be even riskier," Lucy said, taking Mason's cock from her mouth and pushing him backward. He watched as Lucy unzipped her dress, her red lace bra had made

Mason excited all night.

"God you are beautiful," He said, taking off his long sleeve shirt and kicking off his shoes, followed by his jeans.

"Come to Daddy," Mason growled playfully as he grabbed Lucy's hips and pulled her open pussy to his cock. He grabbed himself, rubbing his dick up and down her slit, watching how she took him as he entered her.

"You always fuck me to gently," Lucy said, almost complaining.

"Oh, really? Would you like it better if I fucked you like this?" Mason asked as he held Lucy's right leg in the air, opening her up more to him as he began to fuck her forcefully. As he plowed her, he was surprised that he didn't like fucking her this way, frowning and trying to fight off the feeling.

"What's wrong, Daddy?" Lucy asked as Mason pulled his cock from her and sat down on the edge of the bed. Mason just put his head in his hands and exhaled deeply before running his fingers through his hair and turning to look at her.

"You've ruined me. I don't want to hurt you. I don't even want to fuck you roughly. I want to make love to you. Lucy, I love you," Mason said, surprised at himself for the way his heart thumped in his chest.

"The thought of taking you like a street whore just doesn't turn me on anymore. I want to watch as your pleasure builds, how you wrap your arms around my neck and match my breathing with yours. I want to connect with you, not just dump and run in you," Mason explained, making Lucy wonder how she could have ever been so lucky to find a guy like Mason.

"Are you trying to be everything I have ever dreamt of?" Lucy asked, making him laugh.

"I thought you'd hate that. I mean, we did meet online for a particular type of relationship. I don't know, maybe having you as my little girl made me only want to experience a softer side to life," Mason said, making Lucy laugh.

"A Softer side? Daddy, there's a dead rat in

our basement," Lucy said, referring to the man who Mason had whacked only hours before.

"Yeah, but that doesn't count, that's different. You know how I feel about rats. But with you, it's like I can finally let my guard down, like I can be the man I would be if I worked a 9-5 and we spent 100% of our time worrying about money, like other types of people do," Mason continued as Lucy came to sit next to him.

"So, what now, Daddy?" Lucy asked, her little voice returning as Mason placed his hand on her back and rubbed her affectionately.

"Well, it's time for bathies of course," Mason said, standing up and pulling Lucy into his arms.

Carrying her to the tub, they did their usual bath time routine followed by a new tradition that Lucy had suggested where they had hot chocolate together while Mason read her a bedtime story.

"Daddy. What if we did just run away like the princess in the story?" Lucy asked as Mason tucked her into her crib. He just laughed.

"Lucy. We don't do that in this family," he said before kissing her cheeks and shutting the door behind him as he left her room.

Chapter 15

"Everything is turning out just the way you wanted it," Alfred said to Lucy two weeks later. Over the past 14 days, the state had successfully raided five warehouses, collecting a total of 35Billion dollars' worth of cocaine, guns, and military weapons as well as ending two of the significant drug gangs. Lucy had laughed that it had been so easy, wondering if Mason would have been jealous wishing he would have thought about joining forces.

"You just watch house prices soar as this becomes a *safer* burrow," Mason teased, knowing full well that the neighborhood was no safer now that it was before.

"It's a free market for the Irish now," Mason added, hoping Lucy hadn't just made a colossal mistake.

"It's meant to be; it's a lot easier holding

onto the leash of one dog than it is three. Now they have no competition; there'll be less violence on the streets. A far safer neighborhood," Lucy replied, sipping her coffee and watching the news.

"Oh look, Skye and Sophia are standing together at her Father's landslide victory. How sweet," Ellen said, walking into the room.

"So, where does that leave us with the Italians?" Mason said, turning to face Lucy and giving her one of his serious looks.

"Next time you see Danielle, look at her right hand, I gave her something to think about when she tried to blackmail me into giving her a bigger cut. Greedy bitch," Lucy said, causing Mason to raise his eyebrows, impressed with his baby girl.

"You know, with everyone getting what they want, they'll get bored soon and turn on each other," Alfred said, the warning in his tone almost making Lucy laugh.

"Yes, and that is why I wanted two families on either side of us because when one steps out of line, it's three against two either way. We are the deciding factor, and they can't touch us. Not because we are so tough, but because we are the ones running the play. They can try and do that, but they'll lose. Unfortunately, the state always wins. The most we can do is make them look bad and reshuffle the deck, but we all know it is only a matter of time until the whole thing blows up in our faces and what will we do then?" Lucy asked, looking around to see if anyone could see what would be coming next. Smiling, when she was clearly the only one who could see it.

"We control the underworld. We bring in our own people; we claim this state as ours. We get a stronghold in every single faction of this city, and we hold it with an unwavering fist," Lucy said, taking Mason's hand and holding it in hers. Surprised, he smiled and reached for her diamond collar and tenderly unclasped it, taking it off her neck.

"A lioness should never be tamed. You are wild and free, and I will never try to cage you or tie you to my side. You may come and go as you please, but I have no need to collar you," he said, his eyes going wide when Lucy took the collar and put it back on.

"I choose to be yours. You could never collar me if I didn't want you to anyway, let's not get ahead of ourselves. But I love you, and I love what we are building," Lucy said before standing on her tippy toes and kissing Mason full on the lips.

"But how is this going to fit in with your lecturing at the college. Maybe you should sit this one out and just focus on your work?" Lucy playfully suggested making Mason laugh.

"I have already given them my notice. I'm going to open a photography shop, I think it's more me," Mason replied, nodding as he agreed with himself.

Who is Tina Moore?

Tina Moore has enjoyed the lifestyle of a Mommy Domme for several years. She began exploring kink and BDSM in her youth and found her love of being a strict Mommy Domme in early 2000. Tina Moore is now an author of many MDLG, DDLG and ABDL themed novels.

Follow her on:

Author Page on Amazon

Instagram @tinamoore.kdp

If you enjoyed this book, it would be much appreciated if you leave **a review on Amazon**.